I0609767

SHANE SIMMONS

CRISIS ACTOR

ISBN: 978-1-988954-16-5

Published by Eyestrain Productions
eyestrainproductions.com

The following is a true story.

Except for all the lies.

1

"WHAT'S YOUR PROBLEM?" said the woman sitting at the table that had been set up in the parking lot—the scene of so much carnage and bloodshed.

"Sucking chest wound. One lung already collapsed, the other on the way."

Despite the dire diagnosis, he looked fine, up and about on his own two feet without assistance.

"You're in the line on the left," the woman instructed. "We have about an hour to go before the doctors make the rounds. There's lemonade and soda if you get thirsty. A catering truck will be by with sandwiches later."

"Thanks."

"And you?" she said, turning to the next victim in line. "What's wrong with you?"

"Massive head wound. Fractured skull. Partially exposed brain. I'm pretty much at death's door."

"You line up on the right," he was told. "You heard the rest?"

"Hour wait for the doctors. Lemonade, soda, and sandwiches," reiterated Head-Wound.

"Here's your number," said the woman, handing him a laminated card with "47" printed in large digits.

"I guess this is goodbye," Chest-Wound said to his companion from the queue.

"Yeah," said Head-Wound. "I should be done here soon. I'm betting I'll be one of the first ones declared dead and carted off."

"I'm jealous. I'm probably going to linger for the rest of the day while they try to reinflate my lungs."

"Good luck with that. I hope you make it."

"It could go either way. I'm not getting my hopes up."

They bade each other goodbye and departed for their new assigned lines. They were both declared dead by noon, but the sandwiches were surprisingly good. As early fatalities, they were served lunch ahead of the rest of the wounded and maimed, and the food was better for having not sat out long.

Chest-Wound and Head-Wound ran into each other again at a bus stop, two blocks away from the scene of the disaster. They had both handed in their pre-bloodied and numbered white t-shirts to one of the organizers on the way out. In their anonymous civilian clothes, they almost didn't recognize each other. They compared notes on the day, discussed their choice of sandwich, and exchanged opinions on how valiant the fruitless efforts to save their lives had been.

"I'm Marlon, by the way," said Chest-Wound as the 171 pulled up to the stop and started to let passengers off. "Marlon Demetri."

"Craig Linton," replied Head-Wound, shaking his hand.

They weren't taking the same bus line. Craig was waiting for the 177 that also stopped there.

"Oh hey," said Marlon, as the waiting passengers shuffled forward, climbing the stairs behind the front door of the bus, "did you hear about the plane crash?"

"No," answered Craig, all ears.

"It's going down next Monday. Big one. Nearly three hundred passengers. Most will be dead on impact, but they'll probably try to save some of them. You interested?"

"I'll see if my agent can book a ticket," said Craig, calling after Marlon as he climbed on board and flashed the driver his bus pass. "Thanks for the tip!"

Marlon waved at his fellow death statistic through a window as the bus pulled away.

The chemical-plant explosion hadn't paid much, but at least it was a short day. Now, with an opportunity to get in on a plane crash, things were looking up. Planes paid better, and the catering was a lot nicer than the in-flight meals served on actual flights. Today had proved to be a good day to die. Once he made a call or two, Craig was hoping Monday would be an even better day to die all over again.

2

"I'M TELLING YOU THE TIP IS GOLDEN. There's a plane going down on Monday and I want in."

Craig got on the phone with his agent first thing, as soon as he got home. He was lucky. His agent, Charles Carver, had deigned to take his call. Charles usually let Craig's calls go to the answering service. Fifteen percent of Craig's gigs did not add up to much. Charles had clients doing dinner theatre who were bringing in more.

"Just get me a seat," Craig insisted, when Charles expressed doubt that any such crash was pending. "Window or aisle, I don't care. Find out who's running the show and talk me up. You know my credits."

Craig had been blown up eight times, derailed twice, and involved in a multi-vehicle freeway crash four times now. He'd suffered multiple plagues and diseases, with symptoms that ran from a cough and fever, to a full-body rash that took ten minutes and as many sponges to apply. His survival rate was only running at about thirty percent, but with so many deaths under his belt, he had developed a convincing last gasp and rattle. A plane crash was a rare opportunity, and he'd give it his all if he could get his foot in the door.

"I'll shake a few palm trees and see if any coconuts fall out," Charles assured him. "If there's a plane, it's the first I've heard of it. And if they still need passengers, you'd think they'd put a call out."

"Thanks Charles, let me know what you find."

Craig hung up. He still had a few hours for a shower, a change of clothes, and a bite to eat with Jessica. After that, he'd have to hustle to get to the rally on time. It was rare for him to be double-booked on the same day, but it was an election year, and he had to grab the gigs while they lasted. Primary candidates were dropping out like flies. Soon he'd have to fight all the other potted plants for the scraps.

●　●　●

"Hey, hey!" Jessica chirped when Craig walked into the restaurant and spotted her table.

They were meeting at a Vietnamese restaurant called Faux Bang that was run by Indonesians and mostly served Chinese dishes. The place had been open a few years now and Craig liked it because the bathrooms were still clean. He considered it a good sign that the kitchen might also be filth free.

Jessica got up from her seat to give him a quick hug and kiss.

"I hope you weren't waiting long," Craig apologized.

"How'd it go today?"

"Good," said Craig, taking the seat opposite her. "Flatlined by noon, home by two."

They both ordered a Tonkinese soup with slightly different ingredients and were served shortly.

"I met a guy in the walking-wounded line. He pointed me at a promising gig, provided my lazy agent can actually find out who's in charge and if they're hiring."

"That's great," said Jessica, who didn't really care. "I'm so happy for you," which she wasn't. "Want to know about my day?"

"Absolutely," Craig lied, and spent the rest of the meal tuning out the details of her life and work.

It wasn't that they disliked each other so much as they were profoundly disinterested. Craig was passionate about acting, had been his entire life. He could talk shop about it for hours at a time, and did so with a handful of acting friends who got together every couple of weeks to publicly support each other and privately wish for their peers to fail. Or, at least, not do better than them. Jessica didn't have an artistic bone in her body, didn't grasp the craft, didn't want to. Acting, to her, was something done on film and television by rich beautiful people.

"Those aren't actors," Craig had tried to tell her. "They're movie stars. It's different." But she didn't understand, or didn't listen. It was the same result, regardless. An indifferent blank stare, followed by a change of subject.

The subject Jessica most liked to switch to was her own career, which was something in the tech sector. Craig used to know her job title, used to understand what it involved in some abstract way, but the details slipped his mind as soon as they started sleeping together. Once sex was a given part of their relationship, he didn't feel like he needed to cram for an exam anymore, and everything he'd learned on those initial dates got filed away to the disused parts of his brain.

Officially, socially, sexually, they had been a couple for a year and a half. It still didn't feel like they knew each other at all, but they didn't talk about that part of the relationship for fear it would be the end of it. Craig often thought they should just split up if they were going to keep holding each other emotionally and intimately at arm's length. Other times he thought that's what made their relationship perfect just the way it was.

The waiter came with the bill, and Jessica asked if Craig wanted to check out a movie that evening. There was a new comedy that was a big hit.

"I have a gig at the primaries tonight."

Even if he had been free, he wouldn't have wanted to go. He didn't feel like getting into another argument about how the comedian star, doing a variation of the same character he did for his stand-up routine, was not acting.

"Are you a potted plant?" Jessica asked, once she recalled the correct terminology.

"I wish," said Craig. "No, not this one. Tonight I'm strictly wallpaper."

• • •

He knew the name of the candidate, not the party. Republican or Democrat, it was all the same to him. Only the colour of the pendant he would be given to hold aloft and shake enthusiastically at key moments of a victory or concession speech would be different. The rhetoric from both sides sounded identical— white noise all. He wouldn't be listening to any of it. Instead, he'd be looking for his cues to come from the audience. Being part of a crowd meant following the herd's lead. Cheer the candidate when they cheer, boo the opponent when they boo, and always *always* look glowingly at the man or woman making the speech—like they, and they alone, can offer the change that's so desperately needed, or maintain the status quo that has kept the city, state, or country safe, secure, and prosperous.

The pendants were set out in a cluster of bins by the door. Each paid supporter who streamed through the entrance was expected to take one to help add to the sea of party colours when the cable news networks swung their cameras around for an audience reaction to a particularly inspiring sound bite. Every third devotee was plucked out of the flow of traffic and redirected into another line for special treatment. Craig was among them, and knew he was about to be burdened with an additional prop for the evening.

All the players in the second group were issued homemade support signs that had been mass-produced by a staff of professionals. Each of them was their own little masterpiece of hand-crafted folk art that had been carefully designed to look as grassroots as possible, with quaint, unsophisticated lettering of slogans that ranged from cringingly on-the-nose to slightly clever.

"Mine's misspelled," Craig said of the one he was handed, inspecting it at arm's length.

"It looks more real that way," he was told.

Craig felt it made him look like an idiot, but he took it anyway and did as he was told. It was a three-hour job for fifty dollars cash. Fifty dollars more than most struggling actors would be making at their craft that night.

This gig hadn't come through Craig's agent. It was from one of the placement centres that conjured up crowds on short notice for those who needed to stage an event, emphasis on "staged." Craig felt a touch guilty working off the books like this, but not guilty enough to let Charles know about it and pay him fifteen percent of a lousy fifty bucks for doing nothing.

Craig had his name in with all the major players in the group-dynamics biz, each of them with their own specialty. "Source a Crowd" could fill a room, hall, or stadium with bodies; "RALLY the Troops" could whip a bunch of extras into a frenzy as passionate as you could afford; "The Pro-Test" mustered professionals who would denounce a topic, event, or speaker of your choice; and "Run a Riot" could be relied upon to delegitimize any protest by smashing windows, flipping cars, and throwing things at cops. Arson required an additional surcharge.

"You!" Craig was commanded by one of the wranglers.

He had tried to lose himself in the enthusiastic crowd that had not yet turned on the enthusiasm they were saving for the cameras. Somehow, one of the political-party minions in charge of herding them had picked his face out the field of faces and wanted a word. Craig assumed he was doing something wrong even though, as far as he could tell, he was doing nothing at all.

"Okay," said the wrangler, scanning across the sea of heads and banners, once he had a hold of Craig's arm and was sure the fish he'd caught wouldn't swim off anywhere.

"I'm going to want you on the stage behind our guy," he added at last, after making a lot of complicated calculations about demographics, ethnic diversity, and optics.

Craig knew then that he had just been promoted.

The difference between wallpaper and potted plants was subtle, but vital, like the difference between being an extra and being a *featured* extra on a movie set. Mostly it was a pay-scale thing, but there was a certain prestige among the community for being singled out to be positioned close to the candidate. It raised a player's status from being an anonymous face lost in the crowd, to being an anonymous face earmarked as set decoration for the famous face all eyes would be on.

The key to being a successful potted plant was to never draw attention away from the star. That was accomplished by being safely bland, while subliminally representing a significant percentage of people watching at home. Even if they never consciously realized it, the home audience liked to see themselves on stage. It made them feel like they belonged, and it reassured them that it would feel right to vote for this candidate in November. After all, they would think, some of his supporters look just like me.

Craig was given his mark on stage left. He was happy to see his misspelled placard reassigned to someone else who could look like a dumbass instead. Signs were considered too distracting for the potted plants. They drew the eye away from the candidate and obscured the socio-ethnic-sexual-economic-age demographic of their own face that was there to help weave a tapestry of political inclusion.

Two hours later, once a fraction of the poll results were in and all the major news networks had projected winners, everyone took their places and the party candidate mounted the stage. It was, he conceded, a defeat that evening, but a close one, and the fight would continue in the next state, on the next Super Tuesday, where victory was assured. That was as much as Craig understood of the primary results. He didn't really listen to much else, but nodded along with each solemn promise and earnest statement, cheered when cheering was required, booed and hissed when opposition, hardship, or bad news was mentioned.

"How was I?" Craig asked the wrangler who had recruited him, once the crowd started to break up and go home.

"Oh, fine, fine," the young campaign underling told him dismissively, looking distracted by ten other things he had to deal with on a mental list.

Craig wasn't actually looking for a critique of his work. He knew he had nailed his performance by underperforming it. But he needed an entry point to broach a subject.

"About my pay bump," he began, hoping that would be enough to prompt the man. It was.

"Go talk to Senator Wolcott. He's over there."

Craig saw an older gentleman across the floor of the emptying hall. Senator or not, he wasn't running in this election cycle, and would hardly campaign when he was. His seat was secure, and had been home to his fat ass for decades. Wolcott was surrounded by a phalanx of campaign workers who, on his point-by-point say-so, were dealing with the nitty-gritty of the post-rally chaos. That included paying the potted plants their bonuses.

Craig stepped forward when he saw an opening, cutting through the retinue and straight to the man in charge.

"Hi," he said by way of introduction, "I got moved behind the candidate shortly before the speech, so..."

Wolcott didn't look at him, didn't acknowledge him, but half-heartedly pointed a finger Craig's way and instructed one of his staff, "Deal with this."

"Sir," said a minion, taking Craig by the arm, "if you could just step back, Senator Wolcott is very busy right now."

Craig saw the arm-taker was already leading him towards the door.

"I'm owed more money," Craig began.

"Are you on the list?" he was asked.

"Which list?"

Craig didn't know how many lists there were. They'd have him out the door before his name was found on any of them. Craig took another two steps towards the exit with the man on his arm, feigning compliance, and then abruptly one-eightied and twisted out of his grip so he could swiftly step back to Wolcott's side.

"I was told to come to you about my pay bump. I got promoted to potted plant and I'm owed. You must have seen me right behind the candidate the whole time."

More campaign workers surrounded him, waiting for a single word or gesture from Wolcott to make Craig's departure quicker and more forceful. Instead, the senator broke off from his multitasked duties and took a moment to study Craig's face closely, penetratingly.

"Nope," came the verdict. "Never noticed you."

Craig was taken by both arms this time, one minion on each.

"Well done," Wolcott told him, and then instructed his people, "Pay the man."

Craig was escorted to the exit, firmly but more respectfully this time. He'd been given the Wolcott seal of approval. They took him to an emergency door with a sign that warned an alarm would sound if it opened. They opened it and there was no alarm. One of the campaign people leafed through a thick envelope and counted off several crisp new bills.

"The Senator thanks you for your assistance," he said simply, and handed the money to Craig.

Craig took his bonus payment and allowed himself to be ushered the rest of the way out. The door was pulled shut behind him while he was still counting his cash in the parking lot.

3

"AY, THAT I HAD NOT DONE *a thousand more. Even now I curse the day—and yet, I think, few come within the compass of my curse—wherein I did not some notorious ill, as kill a man or else devise his death, ravish a maid or plot the way to do it, accuse some innocent and forswear myself, set deadly enmity between two friends, make poor men's cattle break their necks, set fire on barns and hay-stacks in the night and bid the owners quench them with their tears. Oft have I digg'd up dead men from their graves and set them upright at their dear friends' doors, even when their sorrows almost were forgot, and on their skins, as on the bark of trees, have with my knife carved in Roman letters, 'Let not your sorrow die though I am dead.' Tut, I have done a thousand dreadful things as willingly as one would kill a fly, and nothing grieves me heartily indeed but that I cannot do ten thousand more."*

The stares across the table, once Craig was done, were uniformly blank.

"What is that?" asked the casting director.

"It's Shakespeare," said Craig.

"Yes, of course," muttered one of the jury on the other side—perhaps the playwright.

"Titus Andronicus," Craig specified, in case in mattered. It didn't.

"Thank you. We'll let you know."

Craig thanked them back, but he already knew.

● ● ●

It had been his third audition that week. Craig consoled himself, as he smashed the department store window, that at least he was hustling.

Giant shards rained down from the frame, and he had to leap back to avoid being hit by any of them. The black jacket was thick enough to protect his arms and body. The hood and mask sheltered his head. But Craig had not been given gloves, and he was worried he might cut himself. It wouldn't have been a concern if he were throwing bricks from a safe distance, but he'd been issued a baseball bat to get his allotment of vandalism done, and that required him to get close. It was fine for smashing headlights and denting the hell out of mailboxes and parking meters, but there were a lot of windows left to break on the street, and Craig was expected to do his fair share.

The audition for the stage play had taken up the whole morning, mostly waiting on an uncomfortable plastic chair with dozens of other hopefuls. The chair didn't breathe at all, and by the time he got inside to deliver his meticulously memorized and practiced piece, Craig's back and butt had been uncomfortably slickened with sweat he hoped hadn't stained right through his clothes. The upcoming play had been billed as literary, though it was noted that a willingness to do on-stage nudity was a requirement. Craig considered dropping his pants while he performed the selection from *Titus Andronicus*, but decided it wouldn't artistically serve the mood of the monologue. Whether it would have made any difference in the outcome or not was academic. There would be no callback.

The protest occupied Craig's afternoon. He had been able to channel his frustrations from the audition into a rousing series of repetitive chants meant to convey public dissatisfaction with a new piece of legislation or, perhaps, outrage at a controversial guest who had been invited to speak at a local university. The chants and the signs had failed to communicate which, and Craig had decided he didn't care enough to ask one of the protesters. Chances were whoever he asked would have been another freelancer like him, with no better idea why they were there beyond their hourly wage. As such, he chose to merely hold up his end of a banner that stretched across the length of the blocked street, and shout obscenities at the counter protesters who had been hired in coordination with another agency to provide opposition. The police were the only ones there to serve a genu-

ine purpose, and were pulling the top salary for their
efforts. Even contrived protests by hired hands could
come to blows when performances became too im-
passioned. The police did their best to keep the two
factions separated, though their efforts throughout
the afternoon were hardly necessary. Things weren't
scheduled to get out of hand until after sunset.

Craig had made it clear to his employers that he
was only available until about 6:00 p.m., at which
point he would have to leave for another job. At the
allotted hour, he handed off his banner pole to a
fellow protester—real or paid he didn't know—and
slipped away to meet with the handlers who were
offering a better wage for the rest of the evening.

Uniforms for the night shift were distributed out
of the back of a truck in a service alley behind the
storefronts they would soon be smashing and looting.
A few retailers were designated arson targets as part
of an insurance scam the acting agency was running
on the side. Craig was relieved when he wasn't issued
a gas can and lighter. The last time he'd been on
arson duty, it had only been a car he had to torch and
he'd botched it. The black Mercedes burned just fine
once he'd broken a window and poured gasoline all
over the upholstery. The problem was it was the
wrong car. Same make, model, and year—but wrong
plates. A couple of numbers and letters were the
same, and Craig had only given it a cursory glance.
What were the odds of a nearly identical car being
parked on the same block, on the same side of the

street, right in the middle of a paid anarchist rebellion? He'd felt awful when his error was pointed out to him, but he didn't even get his pay docked. Mistakes happen, he was told, and the agency had insurance against screwing up insurance fires.

After smashing the display window of a kitchenware store, Craig took a moment to carefully contemplate his looting options. It made for better optics if the smartphone videos of rioters looked chaotic and ill-considered, but he knew from experience it paid to shop smart. If he was clever about it, he might get to keep his loot, in which case it was best not to grab the first thing in sight. He'd learned that a year earlier when he did a smash-and-grab at an electronics store and only come away with a cheap pair of headphones, already discounted. He could have had a television of his choice.

Craig spirited away a high-end espresso machine and took five minutes off from the riot to stash the box in a dumpster where he could retrieve it later. He then hurried back to the fray. At least twenty of his fellow weekend extremists were rocking a bus, trying to tip it. It looked like a diverting challenge, so Craig joined them in the endeavour.

Fifteen minutes after the bus had been felled, resting at a forty-five-degree angle across two parked cars, the only other vehicle to dare enter the warzone arrived on the scene.

Had any other car turned down the street, it would have been swarmed, battered, and turned over.

But not this one. Everybody seemed to know to make way for it. The rioters parted like the Red Sea, even going so far as to drag debris and burning trash cans out of the way so as not to impede the limousine's slow drive-by. The car was in no hurry; the driver pressed forward with assurance and no fear. It felt like an inspection.

As it rolled past him, Craig stopped abusing one of the last pay phones left in the district with his bat and found himself standing almost at attention. The limousine wasn't a rental, it was government issue. Two small steel rods stuck up on either side of the hood and were meant to fly tiny flags of the nation the diplomat or head of state inside represented. There were no flags flying this night. This was an in-cognito outing, even if many in the crowd had already guessed the identity of the passenger who had come to observe their handiwork. The windows of the car were tinted, but not so dark that Craig couldn't make out the distinctive profile of Senator Wolcott in the back seat.

The limo turned the corner at the end of the block and the street filled again in its wake. Having fallen briefly silent for its passage, with only the crackle of the flames to compete with the distant city din, shouts and mayhem resumed as normal, and in seconds it was like the interruption had never occurred.

4

CRAIG SLEPT IN. His anarchist shift had lasted longer than expected. The cops took an hour more than they were supposed to mustering a resistance and clearing the street with riot shields and batons. Craig felt he was owed overtime, but knew it was unlikely he'd see an extra penny above the offered flat rate.

It was a call from Charles that got him out of bed.

"The good news is," Charles said, after barely more than a hello, "I found your plane-crash gig. And it wasn't easy. They're flying this one really low under the radar. No paper trail; off the books. They're not even writing cheques. Cash only, and it's a nice pay-day, too."

"But not for me, right?"

"That's the bad news. They're not hiring. Unless you're an amputee. They need amputees. Can you lose an arm by Monday?"

"Depends how much it pays."

"Two grand, cash money, for one day."

"No shit? Why so high?"

"Somebody has a budget they want to burn through. Probably a government agency, you know how it is. If they don't go over budget, they don't get to ask for more next time around."

"Do you have a location where this is happening?"

"I told you it's not for you."

"What if I can weasel my way in?"

Charles considered the possibility Craig might have a different approach—a way to pitch himself in person if only he could get in front of the right people.

"Then I'd remind you not to forget to send me my cut."

"What's the address?"

"No address," said Charles. "This is happening in an empty lot. You know those old grain silos down by the tracks at the port?"

"You mean the Rummi Silos?"

"Those are the ones."

The "Rummi" tag capped the centre silo in purple and silver letters ten feet high. Rummi was a graffiti artist who had made the rounds about fifteen years earlier, painting his name all over town until he'd ultimately retired, got a job, or switched his street-artist alias to something that wasn't so ubiquitous. In the decade and a half since his heyday, many of his more prominent tags had been painted over, sand-blasted off, or faded by sun, weather, and smog. The silos had been his most ambitious tag, requiring a trapeze-act approach two hundred feet above the gravel ballast of the freight tracks that ran next to the complex. His stylish logo could still be spotted at various points throughout the inner city, but the one at the silos was so prominent, so visible from far away, that the defunct industrial-age grain elevators had all but officially been renamed the Rummi Silos.

The bus line that let Craig off within walking distance of the old port ran once an hour at best. Traffic was sparse at rush hour, and practically non-existent the rest of the time, with only the occasional truck rumbling along the service road. There were newer facilities, starting two miles farther up, that saw heavy traffic whenever a freighter made port. The more venerable section of docks and cranes remained for overflow use, which amounted to just enough shipping to justify not tearing it all down to build luxury waterfront condos.

The site of the plane crash was locked behind the tall port gates. It was some distance past the Rummi tag that Craig used to navigate to the waterway, but he was able to spot it once he was on the service road. A single jumbo-jet wing stuck up out of the cluster of crane cabs, empty cargo containers, and foreman offices—like a hand waving for attention above the sea of heads in a crowd.

Craig briefly considered trying to climb over the fence, into the cordoned-off disaster area, but thought better of it when he saw the pointed steel tongs at the top of each evenly spaced rod. Better, he decided, to try to bullshit his way in legitimately.

"Name?" he was asked, as he approached a pair of staffers at the gate.

"Marlon Demetri," said Craig.

Most of the names on the list were already crossed out and accounted for on the clipboard. Marlon Demetri remained unmarked as being in attendance. A highlighter run through the line fixed that, and Craig was permitted entry with no further inquiry.

The setup for the disaster area was the most elaborate Craig had ever seen. An entire airliner had been trucked onto the site in sections, with each part so unevenly divided, it genuinely looked like it had broken up in an emergency landing that had gone poorly. Scorch marks had been added to simulate fuel burns and strategically eliminate any identification numbers or recognizable remnants of the former carrier's logo. The effect of the crack-up was finalized with a liberal dose of detritus scattered between the various landmark sections, mostly composed of luggage and personal effects, along with serving carts, seats, and the remains of prepared airline meals that would never be served. The only thing yet to be added to complete the effect was the bodies.

Most of the victims of the crash were still lined up in wardrobe and makeup, alive and well until they would be cued for inaction—at which point they would become dead and still. The line went briskly, with enough people on hand to efficiently outfit participants in new clothing, while issuing them bags and tags for their street clothes. Gore effects were added in assembly-line fashion, but were more elaborate than the usual slathering of stage blood. Craig was issued realistic latex viscera that were attached to his body with spirit gum and situated so as to be clearly visible through the tears in the expensive business suit that fit him well. If not for the shredded fabric and all the red stains, he would have been plotting how he might walk off the set with it after the job so he could keep it for formal occasions.

"Do you want me with the scattered bodies around the debris field?" Craig asked, looking around at the crisis actors who were splaying themselves in their assigned positions, and trying to determine where a comfortable spot on the pavement might be had.

"No, you're fuselage," he was told. "Chunk A— the big piece over there. You died in First Class."

"Lucky me," said Craig, hoping he could spend the afternoon draped over a larger and more comfortable chair than the suckers who had died in the back of the plane.

"Seat twenty-three," he was told, and was given an airline ticket marked with the appropriate number and blood spatter. Craig tucked it in his pocket and went to look for the spot where his character had met his fate.

The door to Chunk-A Fuselage was sealed and locked. Craig briefly wondered how he was supposed to get in until he remembered the gaping hole where the nose and cockpit of the plane had been sheared off. The passage was a hazardous tangle of twisted metal and shattered plastic baggage bins, but Craig was able to find some safe footing and make his way down the interior of the giant aluminum tube that had once been part of a sleek aircraft.

Chunk A was inverted for the simulated crash and seat twenty-three was bolted in place overhead. Many of the other chairs had been dislodged and scattered around the upside-down section of the plane, but his remained firmly fixed.

"How the hell am I supposed to get up there?" he asked no one in particular.

"I think you're supposed to just lie underneath it, like your body fell out after the crash," said the closest victim of the disaster.

"I don't know," Craig said, uncertain. "The seatbelt looks intact. I'd probably still be strapped up there if I'd had it on."

"Maybe you were a rebel and ignored the 'fasten seatbelt' sign when the plane took a nosedive."

Craig turned to see who he was talking to and found a young woman, as smartly and bloodily dressed as him, lying in a plush chair that had come to rest in a reasonably upright position. She looked quite cozy, even though there was no leg room. It didn't matter. She had no legs.

"I'm Paula Reece," she said by way of introduction.

"Craig Linton," replied Craig.

She offered her hand for him to shake.

"Pardon me if I don't get up."

Craig bent down to take her hand in his. She was splayed across the better part of two broken First-Class seats. The leg hanging over an arm rest ended prematurely with a stump soaked in stage blood. Another one, resting on a tuft of exposed stuffing, was similarly truncated. The fresh wounds were artificial, but there was no way to fake the limbs that were genuinely missing.

"I heard they were hiring amputees," said Craig.

"They love me for this kind of work," Paula nodded. "I give them two for the price of one."

"So how did you lose your legs?" Craig asked, adding, "If you don't mind me asking."

"Look around you. It was a terrible crash."

"I mean for real."

"I know. I'm kidding. Most people are too embarrassed to ask me straight off what happened, even though they're dying to know. They think they're prying."

"I don't mean to pry."

"Sure you do. It's okay. It's honest. I'm always curious when I meet a fellow amputee. You just know there has to be an interesting story there."

"So what's your interesting amputation story?"

"Car accident, a decade ago."

"That it?"

"That's it."

"That's not an interesting story."

"Sometimes the stories are disappointing," said Paula.

"So in this scenario, where did your legs end up?"

"That's them over there," she said, pointing out a prosthetic pair across the cabin, draped across another crumpled seat and painted red. They were highly realistic, like a carefully crafted mould from a horror film, but Paula had issues with them.

"I'm a bit insulted, really. When I had legs, they were much nicer than those."

"I'm sure they weren't covered in gore, at any rate."

"Even through all the stage blood, I can tell my character had cankles," she observed. "Not flattering. Not one bit."

"So I'm guessing she didn't make it," said Craig.

"Nope," agreed Paula. "She's a goner. There'll be a guy through here who's supposed to hose the place down with my arterial spray. Sorry if you end up lying in the puddle."

"I guess it wasn't so dramatic when you lost your legs for real."

"No. They got crushed by the dash board and the engine block in the head-on. The pressure kept me from bleeding out. There was no saving them, so they were amputated in a nice clean surgical theatre the next day."

"I didn't survive this either," said Craig of the crash that surrounded them.

"I'm so sorry. You must be very choked up about it."

"I've been dead before," he shrugged. "Last time was a chemical-plant explosion."

"What kind of chemicals?" Paula wanted to know.

"I'm not sure. The exploding kind."

"Where you horribly burned?"

"No," said Craig, disappointed. "They didn't have the budget for burn effects. It was a cheap gig compared to this one. I've never been in a plane crash before. I didn't expect them to have a whole real plane."

"They went all-out," Paula agreed. "Any idea why we crashed? Was it a terrorist bomb? I hope it was a bomb."

"They didn't tell me. Why?"

"If it was sudden, then we wouldn't have time to be afraid. We'd just be dead and I could lie here with my resting-bitch-face on. But if it was a mechanical failure and we all knew we were going to crash and die, we'd have plenty of time to panic. In that case, I would have died with a terrified grimace on my face, which is hard to hold for the duration of the simulation."

"The plane looks too intact to have broken up in mid-air. But I'm sure you could get away with resting-bitch-face."

"I like to stay true to my character. Give them their money's worth."

"I get that," said Craig. "But you can't spread yourself too thin. I was going to keep my eyes open and fixed, but I'm guessing this might run long. So I'm only going to do half-open."

"You do you," said Paula. "But I'm going to commit to the grimace. How's this?"

Paula opened her mouth, tightened her jaw, and wrenched her face into a horror of fatalistic terror.

"That'll give me nightmares tonight."

"Really?" she said, glowing. "You're so sweet. It's the nicest thing anyone's ever said about one of my death masks."

"Careful or it might get stuck like that."

"It wouldn't be my most disfiguring scar," said Paula.

"We're starting in five minutes," said one of the victim wranglers, sticking her head into Chunk A and raising her voice so all the dead within could hear her.

Craig sat down and settled into position, lying across the ceiling and one of the overhead baggage compartments that was now underfoot.

"Break a leg," Craig told Paula.

"Done and done," she replied, and did a few exercises to loosen the muscles in her face before flexing into her death-horror again.

The prop master made the rounds a couple of minutes later with a bucket, splashing liberal amounts of stage blood around the cabin before retreating from the offal aftermath. Craig, lying at a low point in the wreckage, felt the viscous fluid settle under his ass and soak straight through his pants and underwear.

It was going to be a long gig, and he would earn his money, ill-gotten or not.

● ● ●

Craig played dead well. It was harder than playing unconscious. In either instance, he needed to control his breath, but it didn't matter if anyone saw him breathe while he was playing unconscious. Catching a corpse sucking air, however, ruined the immersion, spoiled the effect.

The other benefit of merely feigning unconsciousness was that a relatively comfortable position could be selected and muscles relaxed. When dead, Craig was always keen to ask exactly how long he'd been a goner. He would calculate how advanced his rigor mortis should be, and would stiffen accordingly, starting with his hands and feet and working down his extremities to his body core depending on the passage of time. Frequently he would note other crisis actors playing dead and just lying around on the job, some of them openly breathing, none of them taking into account where they should be in terms of rigor or body temperature. Hacks all. Craig stayed in character and never broke. He was a Method corpse. Perhaps not as pure as Paula Reece, who held her shocking visage for the entire operation, but dedicated to his craft just the same.

One by one, the victims of the plane crash were gathered by technicians in biohazard suits and visors, and orderly assembled on the concrete deck of the industrial wharf that had been appropriated for the day's training exercise. The process was conducted more rapidly than Craig would have imagined, and he didn't have to lie in the puddle of blood for as long as he feared he might. Within the hour, he had been collected, carried out of the wreckage, tucked into an unzipped body bag, and tagged with a marker that was strapped around his wrist with an elastic band. He had the distinct impression the trainees were being timed, they were so quick and efficient in their work.

Keeping his eyes half-open had been a wise choice. They remained moist, and Craig was still able to see the world between the slits of his eyelids and through a veil of eyelashes. It was a clouded view, but even frozen in place, he was aware when a car drove onto the lot and parked in front of the field of bodies. He could not only see the car through the haze, he could recognize the make. It was a limousine.

A large man was let out the back. Slowly, this man walked the rows, up and down, one after the other. He surveyed the carnage like a general of old, touring the battlefield after the big push, viewing the many who had died on his orders, and appreciating them as acceptable losses—the calculated cost of winning the war.

At last he arrived in front of Craig and his body bag. Craig's eyes were too squinted for him to make out the features of the face or the jowls that hung before him, but he could guess who it was just the same.

The man threw his arms up and bellowed, "Arise, Lazarus!"

Most of the other nearby corpses twitched, or winced through their sealed pretend-dead eyes. Craig held character.

"Come on," said Wolcott, kicking the sole of Craig's shoe. "Up and at 'em. Don't make me bend down to slap you, I have a bad back."

Craig opened his eyes and looked up at the senator, who appeared delighted to make his acquaintance again.

"Hello, my boy!" he said warmly. "Fancy meeting you here."

Discovered, Craig wasn't sure if his duties were over, or if his job was lost entirely. He sat up, then rose all the way, kicking the body bag off his feet.

"Look at the mess they've made of you," Wolcott said of the makeup and wardrobe choices that had rendered Craig a convincing corpse. "Feeling better now, I hope?"

"It's good to be standing again," said Craig, shaking the simulated rigor mortis out of his limbs.

"We need to talk," said Wolcott. "Walk with me. Even the dead have ears today, and we don't want any nosy people eavesdropping from beyond the grave."

With the senator leading the way, Craig followed him out of the rows of bagged corpses. There were hundreds of them, all fake-dead. None of them were being fake-triaged.

"No one's getting saved," Craig noted. He thought that surely there would be some survivors. Otherwise, what was the point of the quick response time?

"Most plane crashes kill everyone on board," said Wolcott. "Sometimes they don't, even when they should."

"You're not training first-responders," deduced Craig.

"No, we're training the pre-first-responders. Sometimes there's work to be done, jobs to finish, before we can let a bunch of civilian first-responders get a look at what happened."

"I don't understand."

"Good. You shouldn't. Forget I said anything."

"Consider it forgotten."

"I like you. You do good work."

"Thank you."

"You're the right combination of unmemorable and incurious."

"Thanks," Craig reiterated, trying not to give Wolcott's words too much thought.

"I know your face but not your name."

"I'm Marlon Demetri," said Craig.

"Of all the possible names in the world you might have, I know that one doesn't belong to you. Marlon Demetri showed up at the gate a few minutes after you did. And he had proper photo identification with him."

"Is he here now?" Craig asked, looking around. He expected this might happen, and had prepared an apology for poaching Marlon's spot.

"We sent him away. Told him we were full up."

"Why didn't you kick me out instead?"

"You showed initiative. I like initiative. Nobody gets ahead without it."

Craig considered thanking Wolcott for the compliment but decided to keep listening instead.

"And now here you are," Wolcott continued. "Ahead. What are you going to do with your leg up?"

"Collect my two-thousand-dollar acting fee, I guess," said Craig hopefully.

"You'll get your money, don't worry about that. Think bigger. What do you really want?"

"More jobs."

"Good!" exclaimed Wolcott. "Ambition. A work ethic. And how does one pursue more gainful employment?"

"I don't know," said Craig, who didn't, even after years in the business. "Keep my ear to the ground, network with other actors, use my contacts."

"Ah, contacts," nodded Wolcott. "Such as?"

"My agent, for one."

"Agents aren't contacts. They're parasites. Try again."

Craig didn't know what Wolcott was after and remained silent.

"What am I?" Wolcott asked him.

"An elected representative."

"Other than that."

When Craig didn't take another guess, Wolcott enlightened him.

"I'm a man who can make things happen for you. And we're talking, just you and me. In contact, wouldn't you say? Many people wish to bend my ear. They jockey and struggle to make an appointment, get some face time, and never make it past the answering service of my secretary's secretary. Yet here you find yourself, in my coveted company, with my undivided attention. There are men who would kill for what you have right now in this very moment. Don't fuck it up, boy. Consider the next thing you say to me very carefully."

Craig did. What he said next came as a question.

"Do you have anything else for me?"

"I might, I might," Wolcott mulled. "Tell me, can you play a grade-school boy, six to eight years old?"

"Not even with a close shave and a lungful of helium."

Wolcott nodded slowly in agreement.

"Well at least you're honest," he said. "Most actors think they can play anything."

"What do you need a little kid for?" Craig wondered.

"Not just one. A whole busload of them. We're going to push them off a cliff. Tragic school-bus accident, you see."

"You're going to kill a busload of children?"

"Not for real, obviously. The task at hand is hardly worth that much bother. What we need is a bus, smashed to pieces, getting winched up the side of a rocky hill for the cameras, and a bunch of headshots of the victims who were supposed to be inside. Maybe some home-movie file footage of them at a school recital, or somebody's birthday party. Smiling, happy cherubs. So full of life one minute, gone the next. Tragic, heartbreaking."

"But why?"

"There's a representative in Nebraska who owns a stake in a school-bus manufacturer. Unfortunately, his make and model wasn't selected by the school board to shuttle tykes and teenagers around the state. If the company is ever going to land that contract, the board needs to commit to replacing its old fleet. That won't happen unless the current model is seen as unsafe. A dangerous, poorly maintained hazard, poised to cost more precious lives. One staged event later, the ball will get rolling. Pictures of beautiful children, their lives cut short, will appear all over the media. They'll be pinned to a wall at a vigil a week later to remind the outrage mob what happened, in case they missed it or have already forgotten. Social media and talk radio will do the rest. We'll throw in some footage of grief-stricken parents choking back tears long enough to make a statement and a call to action. One or two of those will carry us across the finish line."

It was horrible. Monstrous. Craig had never heard anything so cynical. And he wanted in.

"Maybe I could play one of the grief-stricken parents."

"We can get any number of mother-and-father types from central casting. They're a dime a dozen, and I think we're overpaying at that price point. No, I'd rather keep you in our back pocket for something a little more challenging. If you're up for it, of course."

"Is there something coming up soon? Because I could use the payday. I've been really scrambling lately."

"There are more of these jobs at play than you can possibly know. You won't be the only one recruited here today. I singled you out because I like your moxie. Moxie and moral flexibility. My favourite combination. I'm sure when the next opportunity to do a bit of persuasion presents itself, you'll fit the bill."

"So that's the goal then," Craig said, a greater understanding forming. "Persuasion."

It was at the core of any acting performance. At least that's what Craig had heard acting coaches espouse in how-to books that turned more profit than their acting classes.

"It's what we do," said Wolcott. "We manipulate."

"Is it ethical to be manipulating the public like that?"

"The public?" Wolcott chortled. "No, my boy, we don't waste our time manipulating them. They do a fine job of it themselves. A headline here, a thirty-second piece on the evening news there, a click-bait viral article that makes the rounds on the Web. We have a whole division making memes now. Apparently that's a thing. I keep my nose out of it, stick to what I know. What we do is manipulate reality. Much more of a challenge. Done right, the rest follows and falls into place."

"I see," said Craig, who didn't, but thought the affirming lie sounded better.

As they walked and talked, the two men passed along the outer edge of the deep-water pier that jutted out from the city like a maw of rusty concrete teeth. It saw scant use in the modern era, but the facilities were still functional, and it was called into service from time to time when a big-enough ship made port and needed to be serviced while all the newer high-tech infrastructure was overtaxed. That's when the ancient workhorse got the job done. Today it looked abandoned, forgotten—a suitable place to stage training exercises for theoretical emergencies, where no one would be watching—but tomorrow it could be a hive of activity like the old days never got old, never faded away.

Craig looked at the polluted water over the side—a grey abyss of runoff and untreated sewage. A froth of sickly green foam lapped at the inside edges of the docks, and a film of spilled fuel floated along the surface and caught the light in a spectrum of rainbow colours, all of them toxic. Craig had always thought, if he ever fell into that horrid brew, he wouldn't want someone to throw him a life preserver.

He'd sooner take a bullet then and there and be done with it.

By the time they got back to the gate, the crash victims had been dismissed. Wolcott's car was waiting, and the driver bore the bag with the clothes Craig had arrived in.

"What's your name, son?" Wolcott asked. "Your real name."

"Why?"

"Background check, of course. We'll determine you are who you say you are and make sure there's nothing untoward in your background that might suggest an agenda or an ideology counter to our own. And then you're in. You're not political, are you?"

"Not at all."

"Good! Neither am I."

"But you're a politician."

"Politicians are the least political people out there. Our stands on issues are determined by opinion polls. We choose one of two major parties that are in complete agreement on all important economic and military issues, and then battle it out in public over social issues none of us give two shits about. The illusion of choice is very important. You don't want the public to start questioning the validity of their vote. They might get it in their heads that they don't live in a democracy."

Craig confessed his full legal name like it was a crime. Wolcott nodded his acknowledgement of the whispered secret and got in the back of his car.

With the senator secured in the rear, the driver took the wheel and backed the limousine out of the open gate. Alone in the lot, Craig looked around for anyone else involved in the exercise, but spotted no one. He was the sole soul on the docks.

Craig stripped down to his underwear and left his wardrobe carefully folded on a bare strip of pavement. He peeled his latex wounds off and likewise draped them over the small pile of clothes so they would remain flat and clean.

There was hardly a square inch of his boxer shorts that wasn't dyed red with stage blood. After a moment of consideration, Craig stripped them off as well. Naked and unwitnessed, he pulled on his jeans and went commando. Once he had his shirt on, he stuffed his wet underwear into the clear plastic garment bag and took them away like that, hopeful that a few spin cycles might get all the red out.

5

JESSICA ARRIVED AT CRAIG'S APARTMENT for their Saturday-sex appointment as per usual. Foreplay was generally taken as read, but some token seduction to keep romance alive was in order.

"Espresso?" Craig offered.

The machine still stank vaguely of spoiled Indian food from the dumpster where Craig had stashed it, but so far the beverages it made smelled of nothing but strong coffee.

"You have mail," Jessica said, casually waving around a thick envelope that was neither addressed nor stamped. The upper left corner, reserved for a return address, was only occupied with a hastily scribbled "W."

"It's Saturday," Craig said, remembering he'd already picked up his mail from the last delivery on Friday.

Jessica shrugged and slapped it down on the kitchen counter. It sounded like it had some weight to it. Craig wasn't quite at ease with Jessica collecting his mail, but when he'd given her a spare key to his apartment, he'd also given her one to the mailbox downstairs.

When he finished making Jessica her espresso, Craig peeled open the envelope and peered inside. Twenty crisp Benjamin Franklins looked back at him. Craig had been so excited about the prospect of future employment, he forgot he'd never been paid for his last job. There was no point wondering how Wolcott had tracked him down. Men like Wolcott had resources people like Craig could scarcely guess at, and he hadn't been trying to hide himself. Quite the contrary. Much time and effort was spent on getting himself noticed. Wolcott was the first employer who had been this interested in finding him.

A note with the money said, "There's more where this came from." It also gave the address of a delicatessen around the corner and a meet time that was less than an hour away.

"How do you like your espresso?" Craig asked.

"It's good," nodded Jessica.

"Too good to leave unfinished?"

"You're eager," she said.

"I have an appointment."

The espresso, still hot, was left abandoned in the kitchen as the couple retired to the boudoir. Craig had his shirt off and his pants down within seconds of them entering the room.

"Why are your cock and balls red?" asked Jessica.

After three washes, Craig's boxer shorts remained pink. The same could be said for his ass and other extremities. An hour stewing in Paula Reece's purported plasma had left him marked. Hopefully not for life. At this point, he was willing to throw away his stained underwear. The rest he was more reluctant to part with.

Despite Craig's assurances that it was only dye from a recent gig, Jessica refused to proceed with any further sexual interaction, with or without protection, until Craig got tested. Tested for what, she didn't specify.

With their sex appointment unceremoniously cancelled, Jessica was able to return to her espresso and finish it before it cooled.

"Who's this appointment with?" Jessica asked, downing the last few drops and half-wondering if it was the woman who had given Craig the unsightly pink rash.

"Warren Wolcott," said Craig proudly, like Jessica should recognize the name at once. She almost did. But not quite.

"That sounds familiar," Jessica said. "Haven't I seen him on TV?"

"Maybe."

"He does commercials, doesn't he?"

"Only when he's up for re-election," said Craig, and then hurried her out the door so he could dress well for his meeting.

• • •

Warren Wolcott dealt in odds, likelihoods, and certainties. He measured the odds, calculated what was likely, and then took measures to make sure the outcome was certain. A heavy man, with a bad diet, bad habits, and high blood pressure, he knew a heart attack was in the cards for him, so he took measures to assure it by smoking too much, drinking too much, eating lots of fatty foods, and never exercising. Better, in his mind, to turn the probable into an inevitable rather than sit around for the rest of his life, waiting for it to happen. He couldn't bear the thought of dying of anticipation—or something else entirely—while waiting for the heart attack he knew was coming, if only he could live long enough for it to kill him.

"You're just the sort of actor we like to work with," said Wolcott, within five minutes of Craig joining him over a pastrami sandwich.

"Method?" suggested Craig.

Wolcott shook his head.

"Unknown."

Craig felt a touch incensed.

"I've had plenty of roles. And notices. Good ones!"

"Don't give me your CV, boy," Wolcott said, "you've already been vetted."

But Craig would not be swayed from pitching himself, like he had at many a failed audition, once the writing was on the wall and the door out was already being held open for him.

"I've done Shakespeare. I was in a production of *Richard the Third*."

"Did you play the horse?"

"I played King Richard," Craig proudly announced, and then added, "the Third," in case there was any doubt.

"High school play?"

"It was a small but well-received off-Broadway production."

The play was so off-Broadway, it had been a one-night event in Milwaukee.

"How many people attended?" asked Wolcott. "Don't lie, we can check these things."

Craig thought Wolcott just might, so he was truthful.

"Four," he admitted.

Wolcott chortled.

"I'm full of shit," he said. "There's no way we could check that. Not enough witnesses."

"It was still well-received," Craig told him.

"By your mom and who else?"

The entire audience had been composed of his mother, father, sister, and one aunt. No family or friends from the rest of the thin cast, each filling multiple roles, had shown up. It had been snowing. Mostly he played to his aunt, since she was the closest thing to an impartial observer. After the play, once his folks had congratulated him, his aunt had given him a hug and told him she was so happy that he'd had this opportunity to get the acting bug out of his system.

Craig didn't ever talk about the only other time he'd performed one of The Bard's great soliloquies. It wasn't Shakespeare-in-the-park so much as Shakespeare-in-the-empty-lot. Attendees were encouraged to bring their own deck chair so they wouldn't have to sit in broken glass or dirty needles. The final bloodbath of Hamlet never had a chance to play out for fear of a real bloodbath. Between Acts III and IV, two rival gangs decided the performance was happening on their turf and both had demanded protection money. Being an open-air event, no tickets had been sold, and the only proceeds were garnered by passing around a hat during costume changes, amounting to seven dollars and thirty cents. The entire till was pilfered during the escalating gang incident—either by Rosencrantz or Guildenstern, neither of which was ever seen again—and none of the leads saw so much as a dime. Tempted as he sometimes was to namedrop the fact that he had once appeared in a production of Hamlet, Craig refrained from mentioning it for fear he'd have to specify that he'd been playing Ophelia.

"Out of all the crisis actors on that set, why me?" Craig asked.

"Rest assured, you weren't the only one who got tapped."

"No?"

"No, of course not. We always have something going on. We need actors, and we never run out of uses for them."

"So why have I been singled out for the personal touch?"

"You have a face that screams, 'victim.'"

"Thank you," replied Craig.

"We have something coming up," explained Wolcott. "A big show. We're talking international headlines, footage on all the major news outlets. And I want you to star."

"Me? A star?"

"One that no one's ever heard about!" Wolcott said. "The best kind."

Craig didn't enjoy hearing he was a nobody. He heard it a lot at auditions, and it always stung.

"Won't people recognize me from the campaign rally?" he asked.

"Of course not. You did your job correctly. And nobody ever goes back and looks at old primary speeches once the results are in and the circus is off to the next state. It's bad enough anybody has to sit through that crap once."

Being told he'd done his job correctly was high praise. Portraying a potted plant was harder than it looked, and lots of people, given the opportunity, screw it up. Examples of poor plant choices abounded, and were well known throughout the industry.

There was the kid, picking his nose behind one bible-belt gubernatorial candidate, who ended up stealing his thunder as well as the bumper on the network nightly news. The would-be governor threw in the towel two days later and slunk back to his hometown. Then there was the old man seen yawning throughout one congressman's speech that became fodder for late-night talk-show comedians. It was considered a contributing factor to ending that run for the party nomination a week later. And, of course, there was the particularly enthusiastic supporter with big tits and no bra, who overplayed her part by jumping up and down behind the vice president turned prospective president each time he said something applause-worthy. She had gone viral, and was featured in animated GIFs that were remixed and retweeted endlessly.

No-bra lady's career was over. She had become recognizable and therefore couldn't be reused. Her support for any other candidate at a future rally would be implausible after the showmanship she'd mustered for the vice president. Even though all anybody ever looked at were her giant flapping boobs, the face perched on top of them was no longer an unknown entity. The old yawning man was likewise washed up in the business. Being bored or tired on a job that was all about energy is instant death. The nose-picker had made himself untouchable, at least until he was much older with a matured face. But it didn't matter if he never made a comeback. They were all expendable, and after the damage they'd done by being more engaging than the product that was being sold, their names were mud. A standing army of faces-for-hire waited to replace them. Faces that could be relied upon to be dull, forgettable, but plausible as everyday Americans willing to throw their support behind a viable candidate.

"But this time you want me to be a star?" Craig reiterated, desperately seeking confirmation.

"That's right," said Wolcott.

"An anonymous star?"

"A hitherto unknown," specified the big man.

"Forgettable?"

"Not this time. This time you get to be absolutely unforgettable. I want that sad, victim-face of yours to be burned into the minds of every TV viewer and media consumer across the western world."

"And then I'll be famous?"

"For an entire news cycle. Maybe even a day or two longer."

"What do I need to do?" Craig asked, already knowing he'd agree to anything. Damn near anything.

"Do you love your country?"

"Sure. I guess. Yes," Craig confirmed.

"Would you die for your country?"

"When I say 'love,' I mean 'as a friend.'"

"No one's asking you to lay down your life, boy. Hell, I know you're not a soldier. This is the information age. You can die for your country in all sorts of useful ways without making the ultimate sacrifice. It's no sacrifice at all, really. You'll be well paid to die for us. And the best part is, you'll live to spend it."

"This all sounds..."

"Great, isn't it?"

"I was going to say 'corrupt.'"

"Are you a good Christian?"

"I wouldn't say so, no."

"Then I won't tell you to have faith," said Wolcott. "Are you a patriot?"

"Kind of. I watch the fireworks. I pay taxes. I vote."

"Then do what your country asks of you, and profit."

6

CRAIG'S PHONE WAS RINGING when he let himself back into his apartment. He still directed most of his calls to a landline so he'd never be interrupted in the middle of an audition by a smartphone vibrating in his pants.

The call display said it was Charles. Charles only ever phoned clients on weekdays, but the prospect of scoring a few hundred bucks commission was apparently worth a weekend call.

"How'd that plane-crash job pan out?" was all he wanted to know. "Did you get in?"

"I got in," Craig confirmed. "I also got stiffed."

Charles sounded disappointed but unsurprised.

"That's how cash-only gigs roll. Always make them show you the cash."

Craig was looking right at the cash as he gave the bad news to his agent. With no paperwork to document its existence, there was no need to be honest about the payment ever happening. Not to Charles, nor to the IRS.

"How are my other paying prospects looking?" Craig asked.

"Thin," replied Charles. "It's awfully dead out there. Maybe a few auditions looking for your type, all of them long shots. You have any leads?"

"No," lied Craig.

"Well, go network or something," suggested Charles. "I can't get you all your gigs."

When Craig had first landed an agent, he thought he'd never have to look for work again. It didn't take him long to realize that agents don't get their clients work. They negotiate the terms of the work once the job has been offered. Mostly they email drafts of contracts back and forth until all parties are sick of quibbling and are willing to sign off on some dodgy clauses just to be done with it.

"I'll see who's up for having a cup of coffee with me," said Craig, even though he already knew who he would most like to network with.

● ● ●

Paula Reece had no discernable Web footprint. Facebook didn't know her face, Google didn't know her name. Nothing about her was pinned on Pinterest, and Instagram was an instant dead end. She couldn't have been more invisible if she'd been in the witness protection program. When he finally dug up a phone number for a P. Reece and punched it into his phone, Craig felt like he was selecting lottery-ticket numbers. The chance that this was the winning number seemed about that remote.

"Paula?" asked Craig of the voice who picked up the other end of the line. "Paula Reece?"

"Who is this?"

"It's Craig. We met on the plane."

It would have been simple enough for her to declare it a wrong number and hang up. She didn't.

"How did you get this number?"

"I looked it up in the phone book," Craig admitted.

"They still print those?"

"They do. It's print-on-demand and nobody demands it. But copies are out there if you know where to look."

Craig had a neighbour who was well into her eighties. He took her trash down to the bin in the basement sometimes. When he'd been in her apartment, he'd seen her phone mounted on the wall and noted she must be paying an enormous surcharge to maintain rotary service. It had been an accurate guess that she would have a relatively current phone book. The block of pulp looked big enough to have consumed an entire tree in the printing process.

"Congratulations. You're the third person on Earth to have my number. Just you, my agent, and my mother."

"It's an exclusive club."

"Prove yourself worthy and tell me what you want."

"I want to pick your brain."

"What's in it for me?"

"Coffee?"

"I can make my own damn coffee."

"Dinner, then."

"And a movie," she added, raising the ante.

"Can I pick the movie?"

"No."

"Can I pick the restaurant?"

"I'll make the reservation."

"Choose something nice but not too fancy, okay? I'm a struggling actor."

"Maybe the place I have in mind is hiring waiters."

"That's okay," said Craig. "I might already have a job."

"So what do you need me for?"

"Advice. Maybe. A heads-up. You probably know more about this gig than I do."

● ● ●

"I thought you might be in a wheelchair."

"You thought wrong," said Paula, who walked into the restaurant, twenty minutes late, on her own two feet. The feet, and the legs they were attached to, were made of an alloy metal and plastic combo that were shapely enough to warrant the lace stockings that covered them and disappeared up Paula's dress.

Craig half rose, and briefly considered pulling out Paula's chair for her before thinking better of it. Normally it would be considered good, if antiquated, manners. But he was worried it might seem patronizing, so he left the courtesy at rising out of his seat by six or seven inches as she took hers. The other patrons would have to be watching closely to notice any physical limitation as Paula sat herself down. They weren't.

"Walking around on double prosthetics is a trick," she said, "but you can learn how if you're motivated. Having no legs is good motivation."

Craig let Paula order first, noted how much her meal would cost him, and then chose something half the price for himself.

"I have a confession to make," Craig said after the entrée.

"I'm glad we're out in public then," said Paula.

"I didn't actually land that airplane gig. I took somebody else's spot."

"Shitty thing to do," she said with no judgment.

"I agree," said Craig. "But I was desperate. The point is, I never had the right contacts to get that sort of job. Not at that level."

"But I do," said Paula, who was beginning to understand the point of their dinner date.

"How many jobs have you done for them?"

"Ha!" Paula exclaimed humourlessly. "It depends who the 'them' is."

"Don't you know?"

"All I know is that I get contacted for jobs. Very specialized jobs. The plane crash was busywork because I'm on the list. But the real gigs—the ones that pay more than chump change—they're a rare breed. Has it been the same people hiring me for each of them? Maybe. Or maybe the people who operate in that particular stratosphere swap lists of names. Crisis actors who have been checked out. The ones who have come through for them and know how to keep a low profile. If that list exists, I'm on it, and they get in touch."

"I think I'm being tapped for one of those gigs you mentioned. The rarified ones."

"Then I'm ordering a bottle of wine on you. You're about to get a nice payday. Enjoy it."

"We haven't talked money."

"You don't need to talk money. You'll be taken care of. These people have budgets we mere mortals can scarcely comprehend."

"If you've done multiple jobs for them, you must be rolling in it."

"I've done well," Paula confirmed. "But I save my money. You should, too. These gigs have a shelf life. You'll get played out fast. I might already be done, which is why I was happy to take the plane job when it was offered. It was safely inconspicuous. Anything higher profile and you run the risk of getting spotted by Joe Public, and then things can go very bad."

"I know better than to ask," said Craig. "I'm sure you've signed no end of NDAs."

"I've never signed my name to anything, least of all a non-disclosure."

"Aren't they worried you might talk?"

"No," said Paula. "They aren't. If they want you to shut up about what it was you did for them, what sort of performance you gave, they don't silence you with a court order or a cease-and-desist. They shut you up with a bullet."

"Oh come on!" said Craig, and made a point of laughing like it was funny. He didn't think it was funny.

"Don't believe me then," said Paula. "Work for them and shoot your mouth off. See what happens."

"Are you aware of any other actors who talked and...um...got whacked?"

"Whacked?"

"You know," said Craig, hunting for mobster metaphors. "Rubbed out. Hit. Bumped off."

"The word you're looking for is 'murdered.'"

"Well, are you?"

Paula considered whether she was or not.

"There have been actors," she said, "who were a little too loosey-goosey with their shop talk. I used to see them around all the time right until I didn't.

"And you think they...?" Craig tapered off.

"Legitimately retired on their earnings or buried in a hole somewhere, I couldn't say. But they're gone. And one way or another, they don't work anymore."

"I get the picture," said Craig, not masking his disappointment. "There's nothing you can tell me."

"I can tell you about one personal experience," Paula said. "And the only reason I can tell you about that one is because it already blew up and burned out. Anything I say to you now is purely anecdotal. The people who think it's fishy will always think it's fishy, and the ones who turned a blind eye to it will never give it a second glance."

She waited until the dessert menus arrived and she'd picked out a garish chocolate mousse that was coated in chocolate sauce, sprinkled with chocolate flakes, and came with a side of whipped cream and diabetes.

"It wasn't one gig that burned me, played me out," Paula explained. "It's never just the one. It's always two. Regular actors play multiple roles all the time. We accept Mr. Hollywood flavour-of-the-week as the hero in the car-chase action movie that opens this week, and as the wife-beating heavy in the drama that opens next month in time for awards season. Crisis actors aren't so lucky. Nobody accepts us when we play a new character. And if they remember the old role at all, then we're in the shit."

Paula explained she had done a string of interviews as the purported sister of a mass shooter in an eleven-person killing spree that had never actually happened. Why it was important that so many devout Episcopalians were said to have been gunned down during a sermon was unclear. The incident might have been meant to help push for more gun-control legislation. It might have just as easily been meant to boost the argument for armed security at church events. Either way, it didn't matter to Paula, who had been hired to play the mourning and apologetic sibling of the fictional gunman who had reportedly been shot dead by equally fictional police officers. Since the non-existent gunman was deceased and the non-existent cops were on extended paid leave, the media turned to the non-existent gunman's family for comment. Paula had been provided, and had comported herself admirably. With all her interviews done by satellite, her non-existent legs never drew any attention to her otherwise unremarkable appearance.

It was with too much faith in her anonymity that Paula's employers pressed her into service again a year later when their first choice of crisis actor dropped out of the running. For a single live segment, Paula appeared as part of a group discussion about a murdered freelance journalist who had been killed in a car bombing in Istanbul. Supposedly, she had been a college classmate of the deceased, and knew him well enough to have been at his wedding a dozen years earlier. None of the facts surrounding Paula were the least bit true. Neither were any surrounding the dead reporter. As far as Paula knew, the journalist could have been a construct just as fictional as the character she was playing, despite a media website and a Wikipedia entry claiming he a real person.

The trouble began when Paula's face, on screen for no more than three comments and forty seconds of air time total, rang a bell with a small number of astute news-junkie viewers. In the subsequent days, Paula had been the subject of a long YouTube comments-section debate as to whether or not it was the same person from the two incidents. A nose job between those speaking engagements had confused matters sufficiently for her to have gotten away with it. Viewers saw who they wanted to see, believed what they wanted to believe. Those who recognized her were denounced as paranoid conspiracy theorists. Those who imagined two unique people with similar faces and identical voices were accused of being deluded, gullible sheeple. The entire clash of hot takes lasted roughly seventy-two hours before some other headline inconsistency drew attention away from the crisis-actor doppelgangers, and the entire incident lapsed into obscurity. It was never fully forgotten by the most paranoid of commentators, but it was eclipsed by more egregious examples of wholesale news-outlet lies, and put so far on the back burner that the story was unlikely to ever heat up again.

"After that fiasco, the work slowed down to a crawl," said Paula. "I've had a few decent jobs here and there, but nothing in the public eye. Fingers crossed for something down the road. The stable of reliable actors is small, so maybe they'll get desperate enough to try their luck with me again."

"Sounds like the nose job saved your ass last time," said Craig. "Have you considered more plastic surgery?"

"I have a couple of elective procedures in mind that might extend my shelf life," nodded Paula. "But they're expensive, and it's not an investment I want to commit to unless I'm sure it's going to pay dividends. I might only get one more shot at this, if that, and I want to go as big as I can for that last curtain call, you know?"

Craig knew. He'd never had any sort of curtain call, but it was a dream he clung to.

"Looks like you might be at the entry point now, though," said Paula. "Fresh meat. You could have a very short but very lucrative career ahead of you."

• • •

After Craig settled the bill, he and Paula took their time walking to the theatre. It wasn't that Paula couldn't keep up with her artificial legs. Craig took his time because he wanted to extend his evening with her. He was pretty sure he'd already pumped her for any information relevant to his current career trajectory, but he'd been enjoying the more casual elements of their chat and figured all meaningful conversation would cease once the movie began.

There was no line at the box office. The cinema was a throwback, with only one screen that had spent the better part of a century dodging attempts to split it into a multiplex or convert it into a community centre the community would shun. Its survival depended on the management picking hits that would pack in an audience. Apparently management had chosen the latest amusement poorly.

"I'm glad I stopped by for tickets earlier and beat the rush," said Paula.

There was only one patron lingering under the marquee, waiting for someone. That someone was Paula, who walked right up to him, took his hand, and leaned in for a social air-kiss.

"This is Felix Hinch," she said, introducing the stranger in the hoodie, who looked like he could use a shave, a haircut, and a shower. "He's a fellow thespian."

Unemployed actor was the first thought to cross Craig's mind. *Unemployable actor* was the second. He couldn't recall seeing this Felix in anything and was utterly unsurprised by this fact.

"Formerly of the crisis end of the industry," Paula added.

"Ah," Craig said, suddenly understanding this meeting was not a chance encounter. It also suggested why Felix Hinch was so unfamiliar to him. He may well have already been used up and retired out. But that wasn't the case.

"I didn't last long," confessed Felix, shaking Craig's hand. "Drummed out after I failed the background check. They didn't care for my political beliefs."

"Too conservative?" Craig asked.

"Too enlightened."

"Unfortunately, Felix likes to share his insights a touch too liberally on social media," Paula elaborated.

"I enjoy a good debate," shrugged Felix. "I do commercials now. You might have seen me as the schlubby dad selling toothpaste, or the schlubby boyfriend selling macaroni and cheese, or maybe the schlubby pharmacist who shares some bad insights into feminine hygiene products and gets put in his place by the sassy blonde."

"I usually flip around during commercials," said Craig.

"You didn't miss much. But it's paying work."

"It could pay better if you knew how to shut up on Twitter," Paula pointed out.

"I go back and delete a lot of old posts and tweets if I'm up for a job with a big corporation. But those digital fingerprints linger if they're really motivated to go looking up your rectum for opinions that don't jive with their public image."

"I texted Felix between courses," Paula told Craig. "I thought he might be able to enlighten you on how not to burn bridges."

"Maybe we could all get coffee after the movie," Craig suggested.

"That depends on how well you two hit it off," said Paula. "This third wheel is going to skip."

She handed a pair of printed stubs to Craig.

"Here are your tickets," she said. "It's a rom-com. Total chick flick. You'll both hate it, so you won't mind ignoring it while you talk."

"Don't you want to go, too?" asked Craig.

"I'll wait for Netflix."

She left without another word. Craig watched her back for half a block, the subtle signs of her askew gait only discernable to those in the know. It felt awkward to have Paula ditch him with this stranger so abruptly, and he was at a loss for what to say to fill the empty air. It didn't matter. Felix liked to talk, and the movie that unfolded before them over the next couple of hours could barely get a word in.

There was hardly anyone else in the theatre. *For Love or Honey* had bombed on its opening weekend. This was the second week of its run. There would not be a third. As such, no one was within ten rows to be disturbed by the conversation. Paula was right. Had either of them bothered to pay attention to the film, neither of them would have been drawn in by the paint-by-numbers plot.

Craig didn't get out to see many movies. He preferred the stage over the screen, and trailers over the movies they promoted. Modern trailers told the whole movie in three minutes flat. Watching more than that seemed a waste of time. Occasionally Craig would be compelled to go see some lauded performance in a major motion picture, but even the most Oscar-worthy acting failed to impress. Any hack could get it right given enough takes. Stage actors had to get it right in front of a live audience every single night.

"Do you have any idea who just hired you?" Felix asked, like he knew better than Craig.

He had asked a few questions to get the lowdown on Craig's current employment situation. They had been pointed, as though Felix knew all the answers before Craig could respond. His conclusions seemed to have already been formed long before they ever met. Probably by a factor of years.

"Well, Senator Wolcott seems…"

"Wolcott is a cog in the machine," said Felix, cutting him off. "He may be in the Machiavellian motherfucker club, but they all answer to big letters. Which ones is the question."

Craig had heard of big pharma, big tobacco, big oil. Big letters was a new one.

"None of them cooperate with each other," explained Felix. "They're supposed to be working towards the same goal. National security or some such shit. But that's not their objective. Oh, they're after the same thing all right. But it's a competition, not a joint effort."

Craig had questions, but Felix's flood gates were open, and he was certain he'd get more answers than he'd care to hear if he only closed his mouth and let him vent. Actors don't make for the best audience, but the good ones know when to listen and learn.

"Take the top two," said Felix. "The CIA and the FBI notoriously don't get along. Why should they?

They're rivals. More than they are with any foreign intelligence agency or domestic criminal network. It's the economics of self-preservation. They're both vying for funding from the same pool of resources. And how do they make sure the money keeps flowing? They have to find threats, of course. And if there are no threats out there to deal with, then they need to be invented."

Craig sometimes wondered how many headline news stories weren't just incorrect, but outright phony.

"Fake disasters, fake outbreaks, fake wars," said Felix. "And if you want to fake a war, then you need an army of fake soldiers."

"Isn't there already enough danger in the world?" said Craig. "Why invent more?"

"What do you think would happen if these organizations were actually successful—if they actually accomplished their mission and removed all possible threats to the nation? They'd be congratulated. They'd be given a pat on the back and a shiny medal for a job well done. And the very next quarter, they'd have their budgets slashed. The layoffs would begin and they'd be gutted before the year was out. But if new dangers are discovered, if the occasional attack on the homeland gets through—real or imagined— they keep their fingers on the purse strings and nobody has to go on unemployment. Even better, the budget gets increased and everybody gets a raise. I'd rather have a raise than a shiny medal, wouldn't you?"

"This all sounds a bit crazy-pants," Craig said delicately.

"Okay, let's do a little thought-experiment. How many nations are there?"

"I don't know. Hundreds I guess."

"There are 193 nations in the world today. You can quibble about whether one or two of them qualify as real nations. There's always debate. But 193 is as accurate a total as any. Now, of those individual nations, how many of them have some sort of intelligence agency, or board, or think-tank, or simply a federal police force that gathers information on people?"

"I'm guessing a lot of them."

"Right, probably most. Many of them don't necessarily have a top-notch agency, but a decent-sized nation with a decent-sized GDP is going to invest a certain amount of time and resources into intelligence, right?"

"I guess so."

"Let's skip to what's close-at-hand on the home front. The biggest, brightest star in the marketplace of information. How many intelligence-gathering organizations are there in the United States of America?"

"A bunch."

"Yeah. A bunch. A whole bunch of them. Let's just rattle off some of the alphabet soup, shall we? There's the CIA, FBI, NSA, TSA, DHS, IRS, DEA to name a few of the major players. We'll ignore all the small fish and the privately owned organizations that like to slip their members into powerful government positions whenever they can. In fact, let's just focus on the biggest fish of all. The CIA. How many people do you think are on their payroll?"

"I don't know."

"Nobody does. All we know for sure is that it's thousands. Almost certainly tens of thousands if you count the assets as well."

"Assets?"

"They're not agents. They're people the CIA has under their thumb. Informants, placeholders, inside men. They're all getting a payday, too. So what do you think the annual budget of the CIA is?"

"I don't know that either."

"Right. Nobody does. They're certainly not going to tell you. They keep secrets for a living, their own closest of all. It has to be in the hundreds of millions. Maybe the hundreds of billions. And what they don't squeeze out of the government, they earn running their own sideshows. Drug trafficking mostly. You don't have to believe me, but look up stories about their shenanigans over the years. Everywhere from Afghanistan to Central America. It's been reported on extensively, but it never gets much air time because they have so many people situated in the media who can keep it from becoming the scandal it should be."

"Assets?"

"Exactly. Now you're getting it."

"Okay, fine. So any way you look at it, that's a lot of people and a lot of money."

"And not just any people. The CIA has been hiring the best and the brightest right out of university since their inception in 1947. They have a hell of a lot of very clever people, from the top of the pyramid, all the way down to the bottom. Now, here's my question to you. I want you to think long and hard about it."

"Hit me."

"What the hell do you think they've been doing with all that money and all those big brains for the last seventyish years? Playing tiddlywinks? Or do you think maybe, just maybe, they've been using some of that time and money and intellect to plot? To figure out ways to advance their agenda—brilliant and subtle ways that can't be traced back to them. To plant the stories they want you to hear, to start the wars they want you to fight, and shape the world they want you to live in. You think maybe they're not jerking off in Langley and might, instead, be getting shit done?"

"I guess they probably are."

"Of course they are. And that's just the CIA. Probably the biggest. Probably the best funded. But far from the only group out there and, if we're being honest, not the best of its ilk. There are others that have been running operations for just as long, pulling off masterstrokes compared to anything the CIA has accomplished. But, of course, those are only the operations we can confirm, that you can read about yourself if you dig deep enough. There are plenty of secret ones we'll never know about. The ones we can never know about. The ones that happened because some of these agencies pooled their resources to change the world forever."

"Should I even ask?"

"You don't have to. You've seen it with your own eyes. Everyone has. The greatest magic trick ever performed. Hardly anyone questioned it, no one was able to prove it was a trick at all. Because they were all too busy looking at the staged event instead of what was happening right under their noses. The real agenda all along."

He didn't let Craig think about what that real agenda might be for more than a moment.

"Do you know what the secret to every magic trick is?" he asked.

"Probably more than a top hat with a false bottom."

"It's distraction. Look what I'm doing with my right hand, not my left. Keep your eye on the colourful prop, not what's up my sleeve. Watch my lovely assistant in the skimpy, glittering dress, not the mirrored box she's climbing into. Let the tiger, or the fire, or the puff of smoke draw the audience's eyes away from what you're really doing and you'll get away with it every time. If any dime-store magician understands that, don't you think the overfunded, overstaffed intelligence agencies of the world know it too?"

"What event are we talking about, exactly?" Craig asked, even though he already knew.

"I'm talking about a date that will live in infamy long after that other date that's supposed to live in infamy is forgotten," said Felix. "You watched the laws of physics get suspended for a few hours on live television, and you never questioned it. It was like David Copperfield making the Statue of Liberty disappear, and just as impossible. The only difference is you knew the Copperfield show had to be a trick. You were *told* you'd be watching a magic act right in the television promos for weeks leading up to that performance. But what if no one told you? What if it got sprung on you one day, when you least expected it, and there wasn't some famous magician fronting the show? Would you realize you were watching a trick?"

"What are you going to tell me next?" Craig chuckled. "That Stanley Kubrick faked the moon landings?"

"Don't be ridiculous," said Felix, who sounded insulted.

"Okay, at least now you're sounding rational."

"Kubrick didn't fake the moon landings. Douglas Trumbull did."

"What?"

"If you're going to fake landing on the moon, you don't hire the director of *2001: A Space Odyssey*, you get the guy who did the special effects. What's a director going to do? Direct Neil Armstrong to look impressed by the moon? You can't even see his face behind the astronaut visor! I guess he could have rehearsed him a bit more. Maybe he wouldn't have botched his line."

"What do you mean botched?"

"The first words purportedly spoken on the moon should have ended up on a blooper reel, but they went out live. Armstrong said, 'One small step for man, one giant leap for mankind.'"

"I know. I've heard it a million times."

"Didn't you ever notice it doesn't make any god-damn sense?"

"Not really."

"'Man' and 'mankind' mean the same thing. What he meant to say—what was scripted for him—was 'One small step for a man. *A* man. Just one. Singular. It doesn't mean anything the other way. A quarter of a million miles through the vacuum of space, and he flubs his big moment? Some rocket scientist!"

"You seem to know a lot for one crisis actor who didn't make the grade," Craig commented. "I'm surprised they haven't tried to take you out."

"Oh, they'd love to see me gone, silenced forever. But I'm just one voice on the internet. And I take steps to make sure I'm not low-hanging fruit. If you're a target-of-opportunity, you just make sure that opportunity never comes up. You don't want to tempt them. That's why I never drive in a hackable car and only ever fly big commercial jets. They won't hesitate to arrange an accident if you make it convenient for them."

"How many of these accidents are there?"

"They crash small, privately-owned aircraft all the time. It's called assassination-by-plane. A bit of mechanical tampering in the hangar and the target is reliably dead on impact. Ninety-four-percent certain fatality. One of their assets at the NTSB makes a wrong conclusion about cause-of, files a false report, and it's all forgotten about. Just another tragic accident. Why was so important a man flying himself from Point A to Point B, when he could have hired a professional pilot to make sure he didn't crash into Point C?"

"What's to stop them from crashing a jumbo jet if they want to get you?"

"They never crash an airliner stuffed with hundreds of people just to kill one guy. Policy is, they need at least two targets on board to bring down one of those. For that much collateral damage, they have to justify it by killing two birds with one stone."

"Well that's considerate of them."

"They'll be the first to tell you they're not monsters."

7

EXTRACTING HIMSELF FROM the paranoia of Felix Hinch had taken Craig the entire predictable third act of the movie and all of the end credits. Once he was on a roll, he was determined to unload, and Craig had been the first person willing to listen to him face-to-face rather than from the other end of a Reddit thread.

"People only want to understand politics, world events, and history as well as their confirmation bias will allow them," were Felix's final words of caution, outside again, under the marquee. An usher was up a ladder, changing the letters and show times to a promising new release that couldn't fail to be more successful than the movie they had just ignored for two hours. "To truly understand what's going on, what's gone on in the past, takes time and hard work. And people are, across the board, impatient and lazy."

Craig felt a whole new world had been opened up to him. He wasn't sure if he believed a single word Felix had told him, but Paula's insight seemed genuine, and thus far Senator Wolcott had been the real deal. At least to the tune of two thousand dollars.

Come the following morning and over the whole afternoon, Craig saw reality through a new lens and basked in the glow of knowing something that those around him did not. He felt like he had been initiated into an exclusive club, and possessed a level of knowledge reserved for a select few. At several junctures in his life, Craig had toyed with the idea of getting his thetans checked and becoming a Scientologist. Many movie stars were followers of L. Ron Hubbard, and membership was seen as a prudent upwardly mobile career move. Craig was reasonably sure he could deduct the funds the religion extracted from him as a business expense, but had ultimately decided against provoking a tax audit. Now, he imagined himself enlightened in a way the dull normals were not—like the upper echelons of the Scientology hierarchy did. Or at least those who had never bothered to Google the super-secret science-fiction revelations Hubbard had concocted when he was first forming his cult.

The sense of unique insight began to fade by the time evening approached, yet Craig still felt like a locked door had been opened to him at last.

• • •

By the end of the first week with no further communication, Craig sensed that same door had been slammed shut in his face and double bolted from the other side. He tried calling Paula for reassurance, but found the number was disconnected. Attempts to leave a message for the senator at Wolcott's office never made it any deeper than a government receptionist who gatekept constituent inquiries and complaints for the entire Congress.

Two weeks after his dinner with Paula Reece, it was like the world he'd had his first taste of never existed. Senator Wolcott, an elected official and highly public figure, hadn't made the news in all that time. Not so much as a mention in any capacity related to the ongoing primaries. Even the money Craig had been paid was gone, sacrificed on the altar of petty daily expenses, bills, and groceries.

With his dreams of a big payday and a higher profile vanishing from sight over a horizon Craig knew he could never reach, he grudgingly returned to the gig economy for another low-pay one-shot. Charles made himself useful for a change and booked a training session that would eat up a lot of hours. It filled a gap in Craig's scant schedule that would have otherwise been consumed by more networking with other scrounging actors, accomplishing little and amounting to nothing.

The terrorist bombing in a subway station had proved to be a nightmare scenario. Simulated, but devastating nevertheless. The number of dead and wounded was catastrophic, and the pay was accordingly meagre to account for the sheer volume of crisis actors required to lend credibility to the scene.

"The true horror of a tunnel bombing," Craig was told, as his latest swath of gore makeup was liberally applied, "is that the energy of the blast is constrained. A bomb goes off out in the open and it has plenty of sky to dissipate into. A tunnel like this holds it in, and the energy that gets forced out either end is that much more powerful. That much more deadly."

The makeup artist had taken an interest in physics and scored well on her exams in high school. A flirtation with STEM-field study at university was thwarted by the seduction of a gender-studies scholarship that led, naturally enough, to a job doing hair and makeup for stage and screen productions. It was regular work, but the girl was likely making no more money than Craig was able to pull in as an actor. He pitied her.

"You do much work related to bombs?"

"Only the last four movies I was on," said the girl with the brush and the bucket of realistic entrails.

Craig was briefly reminded of his recent conversation that had ventured into the realm of physics, real versus fictitious. Felix had given Craig his contact information in case he wanted to follow up on anything he had to say. He had considered using it, only to see if Felix knew what had become of Paula, but didn't look forward to getting dragged into another round of conspiracy theories—particularly if they involved unfounded speculation about what might have happened to Paula since they parted ways in front of the movie theatre.

"Explosions like this rip off arms and legs, but we're running low on amputees. Know any?"

"Not really," said Craig.

"Too bad," the makeup artist lamented. "They really lend authenticity to a scenario. I do great work with stumps."

"Less chatter, more blood," she was warned by someone with a supervisor badge and an attitude that was issued with it.

"Heads will roll if we run any more behind schedule," the girl said, once the supervisor had moved on to berate someone else.

"I bet you could do amazing work with a decapitation or two."

"If only!" she sighed. "Fingers crossed for a splatter horror-movie production with a decent budget."

She was quick to apply the final touches and move down the assembly line of victims. Good to go, Craig gathered the exposed bowels spilling out of his shirt and slung a length of latex intestines over his shoulder so he wouldn't trip over them on his way to the set.

"What do you think?" he asked, posing in all his gory splendour, his arms wide. "Am I going to make it?"

"DOA," concluded the artist who had inflicted so many wounds. "Definitely DOA. Sorry, I may have overdone it."

With his fate sealed, Craig went to join the rest of the carnage splayed across the subway platform.

● ● ●

Two more weeks passed before the next bombing. This one made the news. Craig did not participate in it, but watched it unfold on live television with Jessica, who was over as part of their scheduled romantic routine. Craig's red-dye rash had faded enough to give the Saturday-sex date a green light. The post-coital afterglow was dimmed somewhat by the breaking-news event that was going out on all networks across the nation.

The footage was gruesome, visceral, and the broadcaster repeatedly apologized for it being un-edited and shocking. Viewer discretion was sternly advised. But this was no raw footage that was being rushed to air before being properly scrutinized. It was carefully constructed, and precisely coordinated to appear rough and in-the-moment. It was shocking because it had been orchestrated to be just that, and there had been no debate at the network on whether or not to run it. They had their orders.

The aftermath was a scene of carnage much more convincing and camera-ready than any of the training scenarios Craig had worked. This wasn't meant to simulate, it was designed to convince. The burns looked so real you could practically smell them through the screen; the wounds were brutal enough to turn stomachs. Debris was everywhere, windows were blown out, and buildings were scarred with scorch marks. The purported bomb blast had not been contained to a tunnel as in Craig's crisis. This one had gone off in a public square at rush hour and the number of victims, dead and wounded, were being wildly and irresponsibly projected by newsreaders who were well paid to ratchet up drama, fear, and dread. The scene was so convincing, Craig was very nearly sold on it—very nearly found himself believing that some extremist group had done the unthinkable. But then he spotted a familiar face and the illusion was broken.

"Hey, look! It's Paula," he said, pointing out one of the severely injured being wheeled from the site by first responders.

"Oh my God, you know her?" declared Jessica, who questioned none of what she was seeing.

Her hand fell on Craig's arm, a comforting, sympathetic gesture. Given another few moments, she was likely to tell him it was okay to cry.

"Sure," Craig said casually. "She's a work friend."

The blackened tips of shattered tibias and fibulas poked out from under Paula's shredded dress and she looked like she was in shock as a paramedic tried to feed her oxygen through a mask. Tears of pain and panic carved rivers through the soot that covered her face.

"That poor thing! Imagine losing both your legs like that."

Jessica was working towards mustering some of her own tears of compassion as she watched the coverage unfold. Craig stared as intently, but he was only studying the craft.

"She's sure selling it," he said. "Last time she lost her legs, they were cut off in a plane crash."

Jessica didn't understand what Craig was talking about, but leapt to the conclusion he was making some morbid joke of the tragedy. Her hand that had been resting on him comfortingly now slapped his arm in the same spot.

"You're awful! Why would you say anything so horrible?"

"She's fine," Craig assured Jessica. "She really lost her legs ten years ago. And it was a car accident, not a bombing."

"Craig, this is happening right now! This footage is live! These people are suffering!"

"Nah, everybody's fine. It's all stage blood and crocodile tears. I'm sure I've worked with many of the dead and maimed before. I'd recognize more faces if they hadn't been covered in body bags the last time I was on set with them."

Jessica had a basic concept of what Craig's acting career was all about, but she didn't fully understand how deep the crisis-actor trade ran. Neither did Craig, but he was getting a sense of it. And Jessica was lagging far behind. He thought about bringing her up to speed, and wondered if now was a good time. It wasn't. The fight was on, and she wasn't interested in discovering where Craig's callous indifference was coming from.

As Jessica thoroughly berated him, and Craig completely failed to explain himself, the media's estimate of victims doubled and then tripled, with competing coverage raising the bet like a poker table full of stubborn bluffers. The final plausible figure would only be agreed upon somewhere after the initial twenty-four-hour news cycle, once an official tally reined in the absurdist speculation.

By the time the unedited footage had been played dozens of times and was finally reduced to a less graphic, more consumer-friendly edited clip, Jessica was storming out. Her final boisterous denouncement of Craig was replaced by the sombre commentary of pundits who were taking to the air to discuss the ramifications of the day's events, like they possessed some insight into the true purpose of the bombing, or could forecast what was likely to come of it.

By morning, Craig had a clearer memory of what the talking heads had said about the bombing than anything Jessica had shouted at him. Like the pundits however, she could be relied upon to summarize it all in easy-to-digest note form. Such a note was written on a small slip of paper and jammed into the narrow edge of Craig's mailbox where any of his neighbours might have happened upon it before him. He discovered it late in the afternoon on a trip through the lobby to go buy beer.

You are not a good person. You need help. It's over.

It was three individual statements. Craig spent some time staring at the note, trying to decide how many of them he agreed with. The number kept changing as he mulled it over, but was never, even briefly, zero.

As Craig stared at Jessica's final communication with him, his mind wandered back to the bombings—the fake one he had been involved in, and the other fake one that everybody was supposed to think was real. He wondered if he was trapped forever in the rut of dry runs, or if one day he might get his big break and play a role in the main event.

That was the moment his phone rang.

Craig folded Jessica's note into a tiny wedge of paper and stuck it in his pocket, filling his hand with his phone in its place.

"He wants to see you," said the completely unfamiliar voice on the other end of a blocked number.

"Who does?"

"You know."

"Yeah, I guess I do," Craig agreed, like thinking about it hard enough had invoked the call. "Where and when?"

"ASAP. He's in California. Where are you?"

"I'm home. Not in California."

Craig was about as far as he could get from California and still be in the same country.

"Get to California. Right away. You'll receive further instructions there."

"Who's paying for my flight?"

"You are. No paper trail."

"I can't afford a last-minute plane ticket to the west coast."

"You'll be compensated on the back end. Off the books."

"Fine. California it is. I'll grab the first flight I can get once I'm at the airport."

"We'll speak again when you land."

"California is a big place. Should I be shooting for Los Angeles, San Francisco?"

"When you land."

"So no hint where I'm going?"

But the line was already dead.

8

THE MIDDLE OF NOWHERE. As far as Craig was concerned, that's where he was headed.

There's a lot of California, and a lot of nowheres to be found in California. Forests, mountains, deserts. Places that are wilderness, but not part of any nature trail or resort grounds. At least not part of one accessible to the public. Craig was headed somewhere that qualified as a resort of a kind, but not for regular civilians. A certain kind of civilian might know about it, and where to find it, but they couldn't get in. It was exclusive, even though it only saw use for a handful of days each year.

In the good old days, only the attendees knew such a place existed. But then the internet came along and ruined everything. Now, tent-pole summer movies couldn't make their release date before all the spoilers were public knowledge. Likewise, the powerful elite of the world couldn't meet in private anymore. If you were interested in that sort of thing, the times and dates were posted online, often before the one percent of the one percent were told where the meet would happen. Even the Bilderberg Group had given up, admitted they existed, and registered a URL for their home page.

Craig's phone rang while he was still collecting his overnight bag from the luggage carousel. He'd been on the ground for less than ten minutes, but whoever was on the other end of the line knew his plane had landed and that he was a short walk away from the rental agency.

"San Francisco," said the voice. "Good choice. I don't have to put you on a train."

"So I'm close," answered Craig.

"Close enough. Rent a car, get on the 101, and head north. I'll call you on the road."

Craig chose a no-frills rental. He was owed expenses for this trip, but was travelling light and cheap, just in case that reimbursement never materialized. Extracting his compact from airport ground traffic was the hardest leg of the journey, and Craig was worried he'd still be bogged down when the next call came in. But his phone remained silent, as if the man with the directions knew exactly where he was at all times and how well he was progressing.

San Francisco weather is fickle, and can change hour by hour or block by block, but the day was crisp and clear—the view of the bay uninhibited. The whole week had been so agreeable, the suicide hotline boxes spaced at regular intervals along the Golden Gate Bridge had seen no business, and none of the completed lengths of the long-delayed barrier had been challenged by jumpers.

Clearing the bridge, Craig was no more than a minute off the landmark when his phone rang again. He swiped to answer and left it in the cup holder.

"Get off at Cotati and take the 116 west," the caller told him. "You're going to Monte Rio."

"What's in Monte Rio?"

"Trees. And the man who will see you now."

• • •

There were other calls over the next hour, each one closer to the last. Craig was given increasingly specific directions until he was successfully guided to an exact parking spot in a lot at the edge of a woodland preserve. He got out and found himself within sight of a branching road that cut through the towering redwood forest that had first put its roots down a millennium earlier.

"What do I do from here?"

"You walk," said the voice.

"There's a motel," Craig noted of the building across the road from where he was leaving his rental.

"You're not checking in."

The "No Vacancy" sign was lit up, and the "Restaurant Open" sign was off, so Craig moved on, taking the branch. The two lanes became one, and the next road became a narrow passage fit for one car at most, with a slight earthen shoulder to allow the rare traffic to pass should they meet head-to-head. The final branch was designated an avenue, even though it was narrower still, and the woods grew thick on both sides.

Despite the strip of asphalt, Craig felt like he was walking a nature trail. He saw no one until he arrived at an intersection in the maze. A cluster of people were gathered together across from twin signs on either side of a barrier that both redundantly read:

Not a Through Road
No Trespassing

Chanting slogans no one would listen to, and carrying protest placards no one would ever bother to read, the demonstration marched in a tight circle as broad as their modest numbers would allow. After flying across the country, driving to such a remote location, and encountering so small a group, Craig was aston ished to see he knew one of them.

"Felix!" he called out, once he was close enough to be heard without shouting and spoiling the serenity of the woods.

Felix Hinch looked up and lowered his placard that demanded, "No New World Order."

"Craig? No shit! Did you come for the protest?"

"Not really."

"Then what are you doing here?" Felix asked.

"I'm sort of on a business trip," said Craig. "What about you?"

"This is my summer vacation."

"Not big on beaches, huh?"

"Sand and surf can't save the world. I try to stop by The Grove every year to add one more head to the numbers. As you can see, the turnout hasn't been great lately. All the protesters with air miles like to hit Bilderberg instead. Those guys pick a new and exotic location each year. The Bohemians have been up to no good on the same thousand-hectare campsite for nearly a century and a half, so it gets to feel routine after a while."

"Not much to see," noted Craig, looking up at the trees all around them.

"They keep us well back, but the guests have to drive through here. That's when we can make our voices heard and see for ourselves who's attending this year."

"You ever sneak in and have a look around?" Craig asked.

"People have tried. Most fail. Security is tight. They have goons all over these woods. Night vision, heat detectors, you name it. You cross a certain invisible line and they'll be all over you like a hornet nest. I've played with the idea of trying to infiltrate, but I don't want to get arrested. Or disappeared."

Craig and Felix were so busy talking at one corner of the intersecting roads, they failed to see the car coming until the protesters hurried to meet it. The group didn't try to block the vehicle's entrance because it would doubtless bring the wrath of the invisible security agents. Instead, they formed a line and jeered at the car as it passed, shaking their dissenting signage and shouting.

"We know who you are!" said one, bending down to gaze in the windows.

"Fuck you, shadow-government pig!" screeched a girl with revolutionary fervour.

"Fascist nazi shitbag!" opined another.

"Did you see who it was? Did you see who it was?" Felix asked, running over too late to have seen for himself.

"The windows were tinted. I couldn't see if anyone was in there at all," admitted the man who had just assured the occupant that they all knew who he was.

Two of the security detail had come down the road to pull aside the barricades and let the car through. One of them singled Craig out and waved him over.

"I have to go now," Craig excused himself, and began to head towards the gate that remained open for him.

"You have an in?" Felix asked. "How do you have an in?"

Craig ignored him and kept walking. He didn't feel like explaining himself, and was pretty sure he wasn't permitted to anyway.

"Holy shit!" was the last thing he heard from Felix. "Are you one of them?"

• • •

Past a security booth that already knew who Craig was, and valet parking that knew he'd come on foot, lay a parking lot full of big cars with dark windows. His airport rental, off site and away from the luxury rides, would have looked horribly out of place. Craig himself felt like he was sticking out, though no one gave him a second glance once he was past the checkpoints.

He walked the trail alongside middle-aged men in polo shirts and khakis who all seemed to know where they were going. One by one, they veered off individually, or in pairs, heading to their assigned themed campsite. Signs pointed to fanciful places like Stowaway, Lost Angels, and Silverado Squatters. There was no indication of what any of those names referred to or what made a man belong to one or the other. Acting like he knew where he was going only got Craig so far, and finally he faltered and became directionless. It drew attention.

"You look lost," an elder statesman of the woodland hideaway said to him. "First time in The Grove?"

Craig was sure he'd seen this man on television news before. Either as an anchor, or the owner of the entire media conglomerate.

"I'm looking for Senator Wolcott," he said.

"Oh, are you the senator's guest?"

"He invited me, yes," said Craig, wondering if he should offer his name and ultimately deciding against it.

"He's staying in Camp Sempervirens, just over yonder."

The man pointed at a spot farther down the trail.

"You know him?" Craig asked, curious.

"I've interviewed him many times," said the man, and winked. "Softball questions, but sometimes he lets me ask him a real humdinger if we let him know it's coming."

Craig followed the vague directions he'd been given to a campsite nestled in a small clearing that was surrounded on all sides by the ancient wood, and sheltered from any curious drones or aircraft by a high canopy of branches and leaves.

Sempervirens was well populated—rustic, but not wanting for amenities. Roughing it was only as rough as the guests wished it to be. Comfortable cabins with beds and bedding were readily available for those whose idea of camping was anything less than a five-star hotel. The polo/khaki dress code of the entrance and main path was more relaxed here, and the campers were quick to shed any clothing, attitudes, or social norms they found restricting. Some were shirtless. Others pantless. But not Wolcott. The senator was stark naked.

He was seated on a stump next to a fire pit, close enough to warm himself, distant enough to keep any delicate exposed flesh from getting burned.

Craig felt awkward approaching him like this, but he put one foot in front of the other until he was close enough to present himself to his host.

"You can avert your eyes, son. I won't be offended," said Wolcott.

"It's fine," Craig said. "I'm fine."

"You don't have to stare at the goods either."

"I wasn't!"

"Take it easy," Wolcott told him. "I was pulling your leg. There's plenty of trouser meat to gander at, if that's your thing."

"It isn't."

"You sure?" he said. "There's no need to hide your proclivities here. Plenty of straight-and-narrow married men come here in the company of their own personal butt-boy to engage in their annual indulgence. It clears the mind. Or so I'm told. How did you find me?"

"I had to ask around."

"They probably figure you're *my* butt-boy."

"That's not why I'm here," said Craig, quick to add, "right?"

"Don't worry yourself. That's not why I'm naked. I just enjoy the chance to get back to nature and air out my nutsack. You should try it. Nothing like going *au naturel* in the great outdoors."

Craig waited for Wolcott to get to the purpose of their meeting, but he had stopped talking.

"Do we have to be naked for this?" Craig asked at last.

"No," said the senator, and made no move to put his clothes back on.

"Fine," said Craig, unfastening his pants.

He left his clothes in a neatly folded stack next to Wolcott's bedroll and the single suitcase he had been living out of throughout the vacation getaway thus far.

"There," said the senator, once Craig was stripped down, "feel better?"

"No," said Craig.

He had been publicly naked before. Not just at a nude beach with an early girlfriend who was into that sort of thing, but on stage in an avant-garde post-modern one-act play a friend of his had written for a theatre-class final. Craig portrayed a tree, just as he had in his first play in second grade. Mostly it in-volved standing stage left and slowly stretching out his limbs as he grew. There had been fourteen people in the audience, and Craig had inadvertently devel-oped a self-conscious erection with so many eyes on him. Backstage, his playwright friend had earnestly complimented him on his inspired improvisation.

"We let it all hang out here," said Wolcott, as they strolled the vast grounds of The Bohemian Grove and Craig got the grand tour. "The most powerful men in this great nation need a place to relax and un-wind with no judgment."

In his short time on the property, Craig had already recognized a number of congressmen and governors. A new famous or infamous face lay behind every tree in the forest, whenever exposed genitalia and public urination didn't draw attention away from their faces and maintain their anonymity. He was sure he spotted a notorious tech-sector CEO disappear into a pup tent with a lad who looked too young to have a legal drink. They had been clothed at the time, but there was scarcely room for one, and the two men inside would have to press together intimately to fit.

"What do you think?" asked Wolcott, once Craig had had enough time to get his bearings and take it all in.

"I think it's all pretty gay," said Craig, offering an honest assessment.

The senator nodded knowingly, unoffended.

"That's just what Nixon thought," said Wolcott. "Though he expressed it in stronger terms than that. Still, it didn't stop him from making the most important speech of his political career right here."

"The President of the United States made a speech here?"

"Oh, he wasn't president yet. After that speech though… Well, the path was cleared for him, you might say."

"So there's more going on than fun and games."

"Officially, R and R is the purpose of our modest retreat. 'Weaving spiders come not here,' as we say. Having said that, these woods are full of spiders, and many webs get woven. There's so much silk spun, you can get tangled up forever."

"I guess there's a lot of political discussion off the record."

"Oh, more than that," said Wolcott. "This is where the atom bomb was born. That germ of an idea began right where we're standing. Hardly the only bright notion to have been formed here. And not even the most devastating."

Craig wouldn't have been surprised to see any of the Bohemians sporting some sort of cultist robes, but the only person dressed in such attire wasn't real. It was a life-sized wooden carving, standing at the shore of an artificial lake. The clerical figure held an index figure to his lips, beseeching all observers to hold their tongues and remain silent.

"Who's that?"

"Our patron saint," Wolcott said. "John of Nepomuk. He was the saint of Bohemia and knew how to keep a secret. All the way to his grave."

"You've been pretty candid for a member of a secret society," Craig observed.

"I'm afraid secret societies don't get to keep their secrets for long these days. It's all very mysterious until somebody writes a wiki. You can even image-search our shrine now."

"You have a shine? Like a religious shrine?"

"More of a focal point for the closing ceremony, with storage space for the audio equipment and fireworks. You must stay and watch the festivities. It's a real hoot."

Wolcott delivered his invitation like it was the punchline of a joke. Craig wondered if the joke was on him and, as an outsider, he'd be the subject of a human sacrifice on a pagan altar.

"That's him," said Wolcott, pointing across the still water. "That's our boy."

Craig saw at once that the senator's punchline was more of a weak pun. An enormous stone owl sculpture towered atop a tiered stage on the other side of the lake. It was overgrown with moss, and of a crude design that looked more abstract than ancient.

"Impressive, isn't he?"

The figure didn't particularly impress. Craig thought it looked more like a concrete anthropomorphic attraction at some defunct amusement park, left to the mercy of the weather for decades, with no one to maintain it or replenish the paint job. A sad remnant of a bygone era, eclipsed by bigger, better attractions down the road. Ones with moving parts and laser shows, based on a popular licensed character everyone knew from cartoons and video games.

"I'm sure you didn't bring me all the way out here to watch some owl-themed rock-concert."

"We're ready to move ahead with that job I mentioned," said Wolcott. "A very special job. There's a lot riding on it, but I think you'd be a good fit for the part. It's a one-and-done. After this, we'll never be able to use you again, but it's a hell of a swan song. The payday reflects this."

"I'd be done as a crisis actor?"

"Forever."

Craig considered the prospect of packing it in in his thirties. Never acting again, never performing for an audience.

"Is this the sort of payday I can retire on?"

"Not in America," said Wolcott. "But I can point you at some nice little banana republics where you can live like a king for the rest of your days on what you'll make."

"After taxes?"

"The whole point of escaping to a banana republic is to skip paying taxes."

"I've never needed to disappear before."

"We disappear people all the time. Pick out a stretch of grass and I'll fill you in."

● ● ●

Craig sat with the senator on the lawn that ringed the lake, staking out a good view of the owl idol for the show that was set to begin shortly after nightfall. Wolcott was alternately vague and specific about the role he had cast Craig in. He was to play a low-level diplomat, completely fictional but perfectly plausible, captured and victimized by a terrorist group with unreasonable demands and a nefarious agenda. There would be fear and dread to convey, as well as sadness and resignation to his fate. But in the midst of it, an underlying dignity and bravery would reveal itself to inspire others to act and, if need be, go to war in order to avenge him.

Craig wanted to know absolutely everything about this minor bureaucrat he would bring to life before the character got killed off. If this was to be his final role, he wanted to nail it. Wolcott wasn't as concerned about the details. The official documents, summoning this doomed man into existence, with a paper trail leading all the way back to his birth certificate, was still being written. But he did his best to help Craig get a sense of who he was as a person, and invent a personal backstory full of hopes and dreams cut short.

As they talked, the other Bohemians began to converge at the lake and take their seats. Craig was still fleshing out his character when he was interrupted by a booming voice coming over the speakers of a sound system. The ceremony had started. A glossy programme, circulated among the attendees, listed the cast and beats for this year's production of *The Cremation of Care*.

"That voice is familiar," said Craig, as he listened to the introduction.

It had the sort of timbre that suggested it got a lot of narration and voice-over work.

"It should be," said Wolcott. "It's the most trusted man in America. Walter Cronkite."

Craig knew the name well enough, but was too young to have heard him tell the world that that was the way it was, back when the world was still that way.

"He was before my time."

"And this is well after his," said the senator. "But he was nice enough to record this piece for us when he was alive and well and at his most commanding."

"I'm not familiar with this play," said Craig, who liked to be able to quote the classics from memory, but drew the line at actually attending revivals. He was certain a title like "The Cremation of Care" would have stuck in his head if it had been a lesser-known work from a major playwright.

"It's metaphoric," said Wolcott. "Something about burning our troubles and fears in effigy."

Craig nodded. He liked plays to have a strong theme.

"Don't worry, be happy," he summarized.

"Something like that," agreed the senator.

As the show began to unfold, Craig felt inundated with a lot of symbology and allegories, with little plot to go with them. The language was self-consciously archaic, full of "thees," "thous," and "thines" thrown in for good measure. At least the anticipated cultist robes had a part to play, though Craig noted a greater abundance of lederhosen than he expected. By the time Death paddled his way across the lake with the doomed effigy of Dull Care, Craig was more concerned with emptying his bladder than seeing if the whole spectacle had a happy ending.

"Is there a bathroom around here?" Craig asked.

"Let loose as you please," Wolcott said. "Nobody here is shy about it."

Craig had noticed as much, but retained his own personal sense of modesty.

"I think I prefer to go water some bushes."

"As you wish," said the senator. "Mind you don't get eaten alive out there."

"Are there predators in these woods?" Craig wondered, wolves and bears in mind.

"All around you," Wolcott smiled.

Craig got up and made his way to the tree line behind him. The woods were a dark pit past the outer layer of bark, but the climactic fireworks display lit his way well enough. As he relieved himself to a rousing audience sing-along of *When the Saints Go Marching In*, he wondered how the Bohemians hadn't managed to burn the whole forest down yet with their annual pyrotechnics.

"Hey, aim that thing somewhere else!" a voice hissed at his urine stream.

"Felix?" Craig asked the dense foliage.

"Keep your voice down!" the interloper demanded, though the cheering and applause of the crowd at the lake was making their exchange difficult to hear, even between the two of them.

"How did you get in?"

By the look of him, Felix had spent all afternoon running an orienteering course with no map, no compass, and limited success.

"The long way," he said.

The forest had had its way with him, and Felix was covered in scratches, bug bites, and a rash that looked like poison oak.

"You shouldn't be here," Craig told him.

"I'm exactly where I should be! Someone needs to expose these bastards!"

The Cremation of Care wasn't the only thing exposed that evening. Felix noticed Craig had more than his pants down.

"Why are you naked?"

Craig tried to offer an explanation, then realized he didn't have one.

"I don't know."

Craig's uniform, or lack thereof, common among the Bohemians, added more evidence to Felix's hypothesis.

"You're one of them, aren't you?"

"I'm just visiting," Craig assured him.

"Don't turn me in!" Felix pleaded. "They'll kill me for what I've seen!"

There was plenty that was odd, but nothing scandalous about the ceremony. Craig had mostly found it boring and pretentious.

"What did you see?" Craig asked, considering what stranger behaviour Felix might have observed that would put his neck in a noose if discovered.

"Satanism!" he replied, like it was obvious. "Devil worship! Pagan gods!"

"What, you mean the play?"

"Exactly!"

"Sir, this is an invitation-only event on private property. We're going to have to ask you leave now."

One of the ushers had spotted Craig talking to a bush and had come over to see what the problem might be.

"It's too late!" Felix told him, brandishing his phone at the man. "I recorded it all and uploaded it to the cloud! It'll be streaming by morning!"

"I knew you couldn't possibly still be taking a leak," said Senator Wolcott, joining the men at the edge of the clearing. The field was vacating, and Felix Hinch had been making enough of a scene to draw attention. None of the attendees seemed concerned, and the naked ones had not bothered to cover up.

"I apologize for the disturbance, Senator," the usher said, seizing Felix firmly by the arm. "I'm just taking care of a breach in security."

"It's a lot of land," Wolcott reassured him. "Can't have eyes on all of it all of the time."

"You're not going to get away with this! Everyone's going to know what you're up to!" Felix vowed as he was led away down a separate path that ran in the opposite direction of the camp sites. They could still hear him alternately protesting and pleading for his life as Wolcott questioned his guest.

"Friend of yours?"

"I didn't bring him, I swear!" said Craig. "He was already outside when I got here."

"We all know unsavoury characters, my boy. And we know better than to condemn a man for the company he keeps. Guilt by association would hang us all."

"You're not going to…kill him…are you?"

"He's not the first gate-crasher, we've had. And we're not in the habit of executing someone for trying to sneak into the party. It's tempting, of course. You could make a lot of bodies disappear in a forest this big. But nobody here likes to get blood on their hands. Not personally."

"Can you confiscate the video?"

"We're not going to take the man's phone. That would be theft."

"I don't know how the reception is out here," said Craig, wondering where the nearest cell-phone tower might be, "but he may have already uploaded the video of your whole ceremonial-cremation cult thing."

"We'll issue a copyright strike against it and have it pulled down by our friends in The Valley. Handheld footage at this distance in the dark is going to be crap anyway," said Wolcott, with no hint of worry. "So who was that fellow?"

"His name is Felix Hinch. He's a conspiracy theorist."

"Ah, bless them!" said the senator, delighted. "I love to read about all the evil things we're supposed to be up to. They make us sound so much more interesting than we really are."

"He used to be a crisis actor. Like me."

"Washed out, did he?"

"He didn't get very far."

"Then he's nothing like you. You're about to become our biggest success story, so stop selling yourself short," Wolcott scolded him. "Self-deprecation is an abhorrent attempt at false modesty, so put that bad habit behind you at once."

"All right, all right," Craig said. "You don't need to cut my head off."

"Actually," said Wolcott, slapping a hand on Craig's shoulder, "we do."

9

THE SHOOT WAS SCHEDULED for three weeks later in Arizona. If there was a proper soundstage to be had in the backwater town Craig was directed to, this wasn't it. The warehouse was a rental, apparently leased out by a company that didn't particularly care what was done with the property. Soundproofing foam had been sprayed throughout the steel rafters and all down the walls, keeping traffic noise, both air and highway, from infiltrating the space and ruining the recording of live audio. There would be no Foley work, no looping. Everything had to look and sound natural, like an overly produced *cinéma vérité*, heavy on the *cinéma* and devoid of *vérité*.

The costuming department was set up in a loading bay. Craig was offered no makeup—assured, rather, that a natural complexion, blemishes and all, was a must. It wouldn't do for any eagle-eyed viewer to detect an attempt to make a pimple blend in, or reduce an oily sheen on a nose. After his flight, and the usual bother of long lines, crowded terminals, cramped seating, and a long taxi commute, Craig felt haggard. His eyelids were red and baggy from lack of sleep, his nose irritated by the dry canned air of the plane. He would have preferred to get a good night's sleep at the motel before attempting to give a performance on video, but he was told it would be better if he looked stressed and miserable.

"I've done off-Broadway," he said, as he was fitted for an orange jumper specifically designed to look like a bad fit. "I guess this is sort of off-Hollywood."

"Off the map, more like," said the man supervising the fitting.

"Why would terrorists bother to put their captives in orange prison uniforms?" Craig wondered.

"Maybe there was a sale. Maybe they bought in bulk. Who knows, who cares! It meets expectations, and that's what we're trying to do. You need to look like a prisoner. The audience needs to understand at a glance that you're a prisoner. Unarmed, helpless, ready to be slaughtered."

"You sound familiar," Craig noted.

"We spoke on the phone."

"You were the one who gave me directions to The Grove."

"I'm your handler," said the man.

"I have a handler now?"

"You've had a handler since before they were sure you needed handling."

"You've been watching me?"

"Keeping tabs," he specified, leaving the nature of the surveillance non-specific.

"I'm Craig Linton," Craig said, offering his hand.

"I know."

Craig kept his hand extended until the man finally took it—mostly to get him to put it away again.

"And you are?"

"You want a name?"

"It's nice to put a name to a face."

"I'm Bob."

"Is that your real name?"

"No."

"Do you have a last name, Bob?"

"Yes."

"A real one or a fake one?"

"It doesn't matter, you'll never know it."

"Five minutes Mr. Wolcott," said a production assistant, sticking her head through the door for no longer than it took to give a time check.

"Wolcott?" said Craig to the man who wasn't named Bob. "Like Senator Wolcott?"

He responded through gritted teeth.

"Nothing like Senator Wolcott."

"But you're related, right? You must be…his son?"

Craig could tell he'd guessed right. This wasn't a nephew or a cousin or someone twice removed. There was a close family connection. As close as it got.

"Don't think I'm doing this shit work out of family loyalty, and don't think I got the job out of nepotism. I've done my time in Special Forces, and I wasn't happy to be pulled off assignment to babysit some crisis actor who got earmarked for one of my father's schemes. I don't know if he requested me, or if it was the luck of the draw, but here I am in god-damn Arizona, trading one desert shithole for another."

The younger Wolcott had been pacing the room, needing to work out his frustrations physically as well as verbally. While his back was turned, Craig did his research. It took no more than ten seconds.

"Brett Wolcott," he read off the screen in his hand. "Brett Frederick Wolcott."

"Who told you that?"

"Wikipedia," Craig said, holding up his phone so Brett could see. "There's a whole page about your father. It mentions three children. The other two have links, but not you."

"I'm the black sheep," said Brett Wolcott. "May I?"

He held out his hand and Craig passed him his phone for closer inspection. No sooner did Brett take possession of it than he hurled it at the floor, smashing it to pieces. Picking through the remains, he found the SIM card and folded it, snapping it into smaller pieces.

"Two minutes," announced the same production assistant, passing by again.

"Have someone come in and sweep this up," Brett Wolcott ordered her.

"That's my phone," said Craig of the fragments scattered across the floor.

"Was your phone."

Another production assistant, lower in the pecking order than the one who was watching the clock, came in with a broom and a dust pan and set to work cleaning up the mess of shattered glass and plastic.

"Who the hell let him in here with a goddamn phone?" Brett demanded.

"No one asked me to turn it in," said Craig.

"Fucking amateurs," Brett grumbled.

"He has a phone," Craig said of the next man to enter the room. It was Senator Wolcott himself, flipping through some app or other, wrapping up whatever was distracting him so he could move on to the next bit of business on his agenda.

"How's our star?" asked the senator.

"He had a phone," replied his son.

"Who doesn't have a phone on them these days?"

"They missed it at the door."

"Ah well, no matter, no matter," said the senator. "You weren't recording anything or taking pictures, were you?"

"I Googled something," said Craig.

"Something scandalous?"

"Your bio."

"I'm sure nothing classified came up," Wolcott said. "We like to make sure anything juicy gets pushed a few hundred pages down the results, if it comes up at all."

"I was confirming my hunch about your son here."

"What hunch was that?"

"That he was your son."

"Hardly a state secret," said Wolcott. "Everyone knows Brett is in the armed forces. Another branch of public service. It's not unusual that he might be helping out his old man with a personal project on the periphery of government interest."

"So it was you," said Brett, once his father had all but confirmed the truth. "You were the one who requested I be taken off assignment."

"I thought you might enjoy a holiday away from sniping heads in Afghanistan."

"My unit needs me."

"We have drones that are perfectly capable of eliminating targets from three times as far away as any headshot you can manage."

"Your flying tinker toys are very impressive. Until somebody hacks them. Or the target gets under cover. That's when they call me. You can't hack a human."

"Not yet. But I'm sure our R and D boys are working on it."

"Meanwhile, what do we do if somebody was tracking his phone?" Brett said. "Or listening in?"

"You mean other than us?"

"You've been tracking my phone?" Craig asked. "Listening to my private conversations?"

"Don't worry, my boy," the senator said. "We'll set you up with a new phone once we're done here. One with all the latest and greatest spyware."

"This is what we get for running an op out in the boonies," Brett cautioned his father.

"Lax professionalism comes with other benefits."

"Like what?"

"Privacy," said the senator. "We're so far off the map here, nobody in D.C. is going to catch a whiff of what's going on until we're breaking news. Security may be lacking, but Washington leaks like a sieve that's been shot full of holes."

"You need to turn in your phone, too," Brett informed him.

"I'll see to it," said the senator.

"Now."

"I appreciate your attention to detail," Wolcott told his son, "but you're a touch paranoid."

Nevertheless, a hand remained open to receive the contraband, and the elder finally acquiesced. Brett Wolcott accepted his father's reluctantly surrendered phone and ushered it out of the room.

"I can't imagine how I got that way," Brett said, shutting the door behind him.

"The apple didn't fall far from the tree," said the senator once he was alone with Craig. "Of course, the apple proceeded to roll all the way to the Middle East and I've been having a hell of a time bringing it back into the fold ever since. Ready for the big show?"

"I think so," said Craig. "I've been studying the script. What there is of it. But I have a question."

"Have the script with you?"

"No," Craig admitted.

"Good," said Wolcott. "Brett wouldn't like it if you did something foolish like print out a hard copy."

"There was a PDF on my phone," Craig said, looking down at the spot where the device had met its end. The production assistant had done a thorough job of sweeping away all the pieces. There was no trace of it beyond an impact mark on the floor.

"Don't worry," said the senator, producing a backup phone from a pocket in his suit jacket, "I have it here."

"The script didn't mention who it is that's supposed to be murdering me."

The senator swiped down the short document to see if there had been any revisions to the latest draft. One of the gaps in the text had been filled in since he'd last looked at it.

"That part was left blank on purpose," Wolcott said. "Market research was still working it out. Looks like they've come up with 'The Red Fist' as the new insurgency on the block."

Wolcott could see the look of disappointment in Craig's face. He had been hoping to be executed by a more famous name. A top-billed terrorist organization.

"Al-Qaeda and ISIS are played out," he was told. "We have to rebrand the boogieman for each new generation. The same shit in a different package, like a boy-band or a Happy Meal."

A knock on the door told them it was time for Craig to face the cameras. And his fate.

"Show time," said Wolcott brightly. "Nervous?"

"A little," said Craig. No actor ever completely outgrew performance anxiety.

"You'll do fine," he was assured. "Dying is the most natural thing in the world. Most of us manage it without even trying."

• • •

The cast of terrorists was universally dark skinned and dark garbed. Each of them wore a traditional black *thawb* and *bisht*, with a matching head scarf meant to protect them equally from the sun and facial-recognition software. They chatted with each other in English, often with a British accent, suggesting they had been recruited from only a quarter of the world away, not half. Most of them were there to stand stoically in the background and stare fiercely into the camera as one more body was added to the total of their current *jihad*. Craig looked for the lead terrorist who was to play a more active part in the scene and found one wearing a knife on his belt. He was fussing with the wrap over his face, determined to obscure his identity so he could remain in the stable of swarthy go-to actors who were routinely tapped to play terrorist heavies in any number of international action-movie productions.

"Are you Muhammad?" Craig asked him as he approached the set.

None of the terrorists would be referred to by name, but the screenwriter had to call the lead executioner something since he had dialogue to deliver. "Muhammad" had been safely generic, an easy cliché.

"That's the character I'm playing," was the response. "My real name is Maziar Gholami."

Craig could tell Maziar was smiling broadly at him, even under the scarf. He shook his hand warmly.

"I like your accent. Very London stage."

"I went to Cambridge. I'm from Iran originally."

"Are you Muslim?" Craig said, wondering how authentic the casting had been. He had half expected the terrorist cell to be played by a bunch of government-agency stooges in blackface.

"Half," replied Maziar.

"And the other half?"

"Jewish."

"That's an interesting mix."

"My family reunions have a body count."

"I can imagine."

"I'm just kidding," Maziar laughed. "Nobody in my family speaks to each other."

"Mine either," said Craig, who had been told estranged families were the best kind of family to have if you were a crisis actor who was scheduled to vanish without a trace. It would be easy to make the switch from two-minute happy-birthday phone calls and impersonal Christmas cards to no contact at all.

"So you're the one who's going to do the deed?" Craig asked.

"Yeah, I'm the barber."

"The barber?"

"Just a little off the top," said Maziar.

"Do you want to rehearse this?"

"Let's get the blocking down and the choreography straight," agreed Craig's fellow thespian. "But we don't want to go over it too many times. It needs to look spontaneous."

"It's supposed to be a planned execution," Craig reminded him.

"Any first-degree murder is planned, but you never know exactly how it's going to go down until you're in the moment. You can think it over in your head a million times, but the actual deed always has a certain spur-of-the-moment feel to it. We can't lose that."

"Sounds like you've done this before."

"You look like me, you get typecast," Maziar said.

"Ever kill anyone for real?"

"Fuck no. I'm an actor, not a psychopath."

"I just want to make sure you don't get carried away."

"I couldn't kill anyone with this thing," said Maziar, drawing his blade from its sheath to show Craig.

"It certainly looks authentic."

The hunting knife was gigantic. It looked like something that could handily gut the catch of the day or finish off a felled deer.

"It's real enough, but it's been blunted. I wouldn't want to use it to spread butter, let alone cut a throat and then go on to saw off a whole human head."

"How are we going to do this?" Craig asked.

"Get on your knees," Maziar told him.

Craig set himself down into the sand base that had been trucked in days earlier, shovelled onto the soundstage, and then carefully brushed to look like a naturally formed wind-swept dune. The cast had already spoiled much of it with their footprints, but that was fine. It had to look like they had walked to the execution site from some unseen road off-screen.

Craig found himself facing Maziar's cloaked crotch. The same oft-repeated tales of the casting couch had already occurred to them both. As well as the jokes to go with them.

"Turn the other way," said Maziar, gesturing with his knife towards the camera and crew. "You already got the job."

Craig shuffled around on his knees until he was facing away from Maziar, presenting his back for a better angle of attack. Maziar grabbed him firmly by the hair, steadying his head for the incision.

"Is that too rough?" he asked.

"It's fine," said Craig. "Really go for it when the cameras are rolling."

"I don't want to hurt you."

"Your character wants to hurt me, though. He wants to kill me. He's about to open my throat ear to ear, so he's not going to get squeamish about pulling my hair."

As with any other film set Craig had been on or visited, things ran late as everyone in the crew made last-minute changes and fixes in their own corner of the production. The blinding lights were left on, and baked the set under a simulated sun. Craig wasn't tan, but figured his character had likely been held hostage in a dark pit or cave for some time. The lamps wouldn't give him much colour, but were hot enough to make him sweat and lend an authenticity to the desert heat. The backdrop was a green screen and Craig was informed that a convincing cloudless sky would be added in post. The days of blue or green screens making for reasonable but unconvincing process shots were over. With enough money, digital filters, and rendering time, anything could be made to look more real than reality.

"Let's do a take and see what we have," said someone who wasn't the director.

No one seemed to be directing the production. There were only people in charge of guiding it. Everyone who wasn't qualified to make a decision, or couldn't find someone who could make a decision for them, deferred to the Wolcotts.

There was a nod from the senator, mirrored by his son, and that was enough to set things in motion. It was time to do a run-through and see if they could get it in one. The cast stood on their mark. The camera rolled, even though there was nothing to roll through modern camera equipment, and the scene unfolded as scripted. Everyone was on edge, and it lent a certain energy to the performances that would be impossible to recreate in subsequent takes.

Craig barely heard the posturing of his extremist captor, even though he'd read the lines many times. He, himself, had no dialogue to deliver beyond a gurgling, pained reaction to getting his throat cut. The whole time he was focused on the cold steel poised at his throat. His character, he imagined, would be thinking of nothing else in the moment.

Maziar performed his monologue in heavily accented and semi-broken English that sounded nothing like him at all. He listed off the terrorist cell's demands, carefully composed to be plausible yet unrealistic—utterly impossible to meet. There was no room for negotiation, and they were about to recklessly throw away their one bargaining chip, vowing to kidnap and murder more if their cause wasn't taken more seriously by the infidels within western governments.

At last it was time for Craig to be made an example of. Maziar pulled his hair twice as hard as he had in rehearsal and proceeded to saw at his throat with the blunt edge of his knife. It was hard enough to leave a temporary mark but, as promised, the knife was so blunt it couldn't do more than indent Craig's flesh.

"Cut!" was called from a distant corner of the soundstage by someone who knew what they were doing, and the blunted sawing ceased. Maziar released Craig's hair and gave him a playful slap across the back of the head.

"Good show!" he commended in his regular accent. "You die well."

"Comes with experience," Craig said.

"Intense as ever, Mr. Gholami," Senator Wolcott told Maziar, as he approached to congratulate his cast. "You really put the fear of Allah in me."

"Thank you, sir," nodded Maziar humbly, "thank you."

"If only my childhood pastor had been such a firebrand, I think he would have scared the sin right out of me."

"Is that it?" asked Craig. "Are we done already?"

It felt anticlimactic after weeks of mystery and build-up.

Wolcott was given the thumbs up by his camera operator and the sound technician as both men ran through their playback and confirmed there had been no technical glitch on their end that might compromise the final product.

"We're good," announced the senator.

"You sure you don't want to do another take?"

"We'll never get it that raw again," said Wolcott. "No, I'd say we're one and done. What do you think Mr. DeMille?"

"Don't ask me," said Brett. "I just work here."

"I thought there would be more to it," said Craig. "Especially if we were getting it all in one shot."

He hadn't expected the single shot to be as elaborate as the long-take novelty shots of a Welles or an Altman, but he'd figured there might be a twist to their secretive efforts in Arizona.

"You didn't think we were really going to kill you?" chuckled Wolcott.

"Of course not."

"We need you alive and well for the interview."

"There's an interview?"

It was news to Craig.

"You're going under the knife again. Or rather, the razor this time. A fresh shave, some makeup, and you'll look like your old self. Or the old self you were supposed to be before your tragic kidnapping and murder."

• • •

Over the course of the next hour, Craig was given a haircut and shave and prepped for a live interview that was going out over a satellite dish that had been installed on the roof of the warehouse a week earlier. Aside from makeup and hair, the prep involved grilling Craig about the basic biography of the deceased diplomat he'd been hired to play. Anticipating the role, he had already imagined all sorts of stories and anecdotes about his character's life, but there had also been a long list of dry facts to memorize leading up to the day's shoot. They had come on a two-page rider that had been affixed to the end of the script, and matched the paperwork that had been filed and planted to bring the character to life from the government-bureaucracy side of reality.

"None of this shit's going to come up in the interview," Craig was assured by the production assistant, who went over various dates and locations of life events like a high school teacher delivering a pop quiz. "But just in case some random point of personal trivia gets mentioned, it's better if you don't look like you've been caught off guard."

The interview was with one of the twenty-four-hour news networks. Craig had already forgotten which one he would be speaking to. They had all blended together in his mind as one amorphous blob of talking points and punditry. He was supposed to be doing a brief Skype call about his new assignment overseas, offering his professional assessment of the situation at his post in a country most of the viewers would never have heard of. Craig was aware of what his character's opinion was supposed to be. His job was to put it into words that sounded like natural conversation. As such, they hadn't been scripted, and he was expected to improvise.

"Don't worry," he was told. "If we see you fucking it up, we've got someone ready to cut the feed due to technical problems."

The interview segment would be brief and vacuous by design. Viewers who saw it would mostly do so at airports and gyms with the sound down. The whole point was to have some frames of footage and maybe a short sound bite on file that could be played later, once his terrible fate had been announced to the world, in order to present context of who the victim had been in better times.

Once he'd been made up and outfitted in nice but casual clothes, Craig was shown to another set inside the warehouse. A small section had been blocked off to create two walls of what, from the camera's view-point, looked like a homey living room in suburbia. In the name of authenticity, the shoot would be done with the webcam of an actual laptop. The laptop, however, was firmly locked down on a heavy mount in a low position that suggested it sat casually upon a coffee table. It was essential that, during the live segment, it could not be jostled in any way that might budge the carefully framed shot and reveal that the living room was no more than plastered and painted plywood, with few props and no ceiling.

Craig set himself down on the couch that had been carefully selected to match the decor, and similarly affixed in a camera-friendly spot, with the legs nailed to the floorboards of the raised stage. Framed family photos had been hot glued to the wall, and nothing short of a magnitude-nine earthquake on the Richter scale could dislodge them. They would be burned with the rest of the set once their purpose had been served. A number of other props were kept off stage for last-minute set dressing if they were deemed necessary to make the space look more lived in once Craig was in place. When the final position of his head in the shot was known, a few books on the shelf behind him were rearranged so the most character-relevant spines could be read. An additional IKEA floor lamp was brought in to stand next to the couch and provide a more plausible light source for the set that had already been lit to look like an unprofessionally illuminated house interior.

Precisely at the allotted time, Craig was welcomed by the host of a low-rated international affairs show that, for half an hour each week, became the sacrificial lamb of air time devoted to what was happening in the rest of the world outside the borders of the United States and its various holdings. She appeared in a small window in the upper corner of the laptop. Craig's own image took up the rest of the real estate of the screen, since it was more important he keep himself properly centred than to engage with the host.

As television segments went, this one was particularly brief, with viewer interest calculated to extend, at most, three minutes. The questions were as innocuous and banal as Craig could have hoped, and he wondered if the interviewer was operating from an assigned script of her own. Just as he was coached, Craig answered each query with vagaries and platitudes. He spoke authoritatively about a corner of the world he'd never been to and hoped to never see, getting into the sort of detail that would fill time without offering actual insight or value.

Just as he was delving into the cultural challenges of an ethnicity he had never encountered, Craig heard a sudden clunk and clatter behind him. He resisted the urge to turn around to see what it was, then second guessed himself and wondered if it looked odd for him not to react to something that may have just happened on camera, and had certainly been picked up by the audio feed.

Like a veteran of the stage, and all the errors and distractions that were likely to crop up during a performance, Craig powered through the awkward moment and successfully wrapped up the interview no more than forty seconds later. Only after he had been thanked for his time and his expertise, and the feed had gone dark, did he dare turn around to see what had happened.

"The lamp fell over," he said, noting the one change to the set behind him.

"So it did," sighed Senator Wolcott. "The pitfalls of hasty set design."

"Should I have acknowledged it?"

"Maybe, maybe not. You got through the interview. That's what's important."

"Won't it look odd? A lamp that was supposed to be standing there for years, waiting until we were on live television to fall over?"

Years of experience had made Wolcott resigned to such imperfections cropping up in even the best-planned scenarios. And this was not his finest work.

"It will give the conspiracy theorists something to talk about after you get killed."

"When does that happen?" Craig wondered.

"You meet your tragic demise two weeks from now. At least as far as the rest of the world is concerned. An hour ago in real time."

"What do I do until then?"

"You'll lie low and relax."

"What if somebody recognizes me?" asked Craig.

"They won't," Wolcott assured him. "You're nobody."

"But maybe after the fact, once the execution video goes out."

"They won't be looking at you. They'll all be looking at the man in the mask doing the deed."

"Even though they can't see his face?"

"*Because* they can't see his face. They're going to be looking at his eyes, trying to imagine the rest of his face. They won't be able to focus anywhere else."

"Upstaged again," Craig lamented. "The story of my life."

"Now it's the story of your death. Be glad it's also the story of your lucrative retirement."

"Still, somebody might spot me. Pick me out of a crowd. Make the connection."

"Grow a moustache."

"I can grow a full beard," Craig suggested.

"Don't grow a beard," advised the senator. "Beards look like you have something to hide. Grow a moustache. Moustaches are repulsive. People naturally turn away, avert their eyes. A moustache is the perfect disguise."

"Where am I supposed to lie low and relax?" Craig asked, hoping that if he had to hole up in a hotel room, it would be one with fast internet, satellite TV, and a room-service menu that wouldn't get repetitive after the first few days.

"You're leaving for Bahrain tonight," he was informed.

"What's in Bahrain?" asked Craig, unsure if he could even find it on a map. Less sure he'd be looking in the correct hemisphere.

"Beaches mostly," said Wolcott. "You'll enjoy it. It's like a Club Med. A Club Med in the Persian Gulf."

Everything Craig knew about the Persian Gulf came from war coverage that had run in a loop all through his childhood, like Saturday-morning cartoons and prime-time sitcoms. The senator's choice of where to stash him until the story they had just concocted finally dropped out of the news cycle undoubtedly reflected his broader interests.

"It's always about oil, isn't it?" Craig said knowingly. But he didn't know at all.

"Oil? Please!" scoffed Wolcott. "Take it from this old fossil, oil has had its day. Bahrain has moved beyond that. They're looking towards the future."

"What future is that?"

"Banking. The petrodollar isn't worth a damn without banks to keep the black gold flowing."

"So it's money," nodded Craig, like this time he knew for certain.

"Boy, it's always about the money. There's nothing special about the money in Bahrain, but you might as well sit on a sandy beach while you're counting your cash. Bahrain offers a brisk tourist trade. Plus plenty of off-shore banking options for those wealthy tourists, of course. You're one of them now."

"If it's not oil or money that put Bahrain on the map, what is it then?"

"It's their airfield. A nice strip of tarmac that makes for a short bombing-commute to Yemen."

"What did Yemen do?"

"It got in the way."

"How long do I stay in Bahrain?" asked Craig.

"Give it a month," said Wolcott. "After that, go wherever you please."

"Any recommendations?"

The senator gave Craig's question careful consideration for a few seconds.

"Stay the hell out of Yemen. The Yemenis wish they could."

10

THERE WAS NO NEED to travel to Bahrain incognito. Craig Linton was free to go anywhere as himself. The interview had been so boring, no one was likely to have paid it any heed. And the world was still weeks away from knowing his face as a high-profile terrorist victim. For the moment, he didn't have to make himself scarce, didn't have to wear a hat and shades indoors to avoid curious stares and possible recognition.

Direct flights to the international airport in Muharraq were scarce, but Craig was able to book a connection through Amsterdam with KLM. He wasn't staying in the capital city of Manama. A more remote spot awaited him at the man-made atoll of Durrat Al Bahrain in the south. The interconnected islands were laid out in a series of fish-shaped plots of land and narrow semi-circles that offered the maximum possible amount of beachfront and marina property to go with the highest possible property values.

The taxi trip through barren, yellow landscape was uneventful, and the driver was quite chatty about all the wonderful cultural events and festivals his tiny nation had to offer. Craig was there at precisely the wrong time of year to catch any of them, but he let the man kill the commute with his prideful patriotism.

There was a hotel room waiting for him at the end of his journey. Craig hadn't been comped a suite, but it was a nice room just the same, with a good view of the sculpted waterfront that was beautiful but overdesigned, and couldn't possibly look less natural. Once the sun was low enough to not burn him to a crisp, he headed out to walk as much of it as he could before having to decide where to eat. His vacation in exile was, he decided, off to a splendid start.

The beaches were filled with attractive people, immodestly dressed and obviously not local. More than a few specimens of shapely legs and perky asses caught his attention, and Craig wondered how much he might be able to indulge his newly single status during this hiatus from the rest of his life.

It was an hour into his walk when one particular pair of legs, stretched across a collapsible canopy chair, caught his eye. The legs were tanned and truncated, with the stumps poking out from under a flowery skirt. Craig recognized them before his eyes ever made it to the familiar face hiding under a pair of oversized sunglasses.

"Those wounds healed quickly. You'd never guess this just happened."

Paula Reece tipped her glasses forward so she could take an unobstructed look at the man who had spotted her on her sabbatical.

"Momma's old family cure for what ails," she said, toasting him with her glass of iced tea. "Lots of chicken soup and Bactine."

"This seat taken?" Craig asked of the twin next to Paula's.

"Yeah," she said, "but you can move the girls. They won't mind."

The chair was occupied by Paula's pair of prosthetics. Craig set them aside and sat down.

"I saw you on the news," he said.

"How did I look?"

"Mortally wounded."

"I pulled through."

"In style."

"And well compensated," Paula said. "They've had me set up at a lovely villa since the day I got blown up."

"A villa no less?" whistled Craig. "All I got was a crappy hotel room. I mean, it's very nice, but it's no villa."

"I haven't seen you turn up dead yet," said Paula. "Not that I'm keeping tabs on current events. There's too much tanning to do to bother watching cable news."

"My tragic end hasn't aired yet," said Craig. "Last I heard, I have another twelve days to live."

"We should have a screening when it happens," suggested Paula. "Make a party of it. There's an eighty-inch super high-def monster at my place that's just going to waste. So far I've only watched one set of tennis and a single syndicated rerun of *Friends* in Farsi. I'd love to see you die in some ghastly accident."

"Actually, I got murdered."

"Even better!" Paula exclaimed. "Was it really gruesome?"

"They cut my head off."

"Lucky!" she said, and sounded genuinely jealous.

"The video ends early so you don't really see anything. It's suggested, not shown."

"Hitchcockian," she nodded knowingly. "Classy."

"So is that an official invite over to your place?"

"It might be."

"You hardly know me."

"Twelve days can change that."

"So what do we do today while we're still practically strangers?"

"You're the one who just died and went to heaven. You choose."

"I could use a drink," Craig decided.

"Then you've come to the right Muslim country," said Paula. "Bahrain isn't as dry as the rest of the Middle East. We can get a drink in any hotel bar. Just don't try to stumble home after. They'll toss you behind bars if they catch you drunk in public."

"You sound like you have first-hand experience."

"I had a close call when I first got here. I was indulging myself on the flight and tried to keep my buzz going once the taxi dropped me off. Nearly didn't make it to the villa. Almost got detoured to jail."

"They let you go with a warning?"

"I played the crippled-girl card. It went a long way towards explaining why I was stumbling around."

Paula didn't stumble on her artificial legs at all, but the security men working the Durrat Al Bahrain beat didn't know that. Craig would have loved to have seen their faces when Paula hitched up her dress enough to show them she was getting around on not one but two prosthetics.

"Have you figured out your favourite place to get drunk yet?" Craig asked.

Paula's smile assured him she had.

"Let me grab my gams and we'll go," she said.

• • •

No one had asked Craig to sign a non-disclosure agreement for his final crisis-actor gig, but he had taken it as a given that the job was not to be discussed with anyone, ever, under any circumstances. His lips had remained firmly sealed, like a tomb of the ancients, right up until he was chewing on the olive from his third vodka martini. Then the dam burst and shop talk came flowing out. Paula was equally indiscreet about her spectacular last bow.

"The bone shards they stuck on the end of my legs were real bone," she told him.

"Human bone?" Craig wondered.

"Oh, yeah," she said. "No expense spared. You never know who's watching out there in TV Land. You try to get away with animal bones, somebody's going to spot it and start a meme. No, the F/X guy told me he picked out a couple of real ones at a medical supply facility. He broke off the ends by smashing them against a cinderblock so the fractures would look authentic, then he scorched them with a blowtorch and splashed them with stage blood. They only aired the unedited footage for the first couple of hours after the story broke. After that, the broadcasters blurred the footage so they could pretend they were being tasteful. You can still see the hard-R version online. It's a quality gore effect, very old-school, '80s horror. Not like all that CG-cartoon splatter crap they do now."

Craig was no less candid about his experience with the end-game gig he'd been assigned. Their shared secrets amounted to mutually assured destruction. Told in confidence, one crisis actor to another, they could do no harm unless they wanted to face equal admonishments from disapproving bosses who might seek a more permanent means of assuring their future non-disclosures.

The more rounds they went through, the more flirtatious Craig became. He wasn't in seduction mode as such, but the charm offensive was in full swing. It was a mode working actors could turn on and off at will, and was a key tool to keep them working. Paula caught on immediately, and leapt to the logical conclusion since she was certainly in no position to offer him work. Neither of them ever needed to work again following their final big paydays.

"A few drinks and you think I'm going to spread my stumps for you?" she asked with a sly grin.

"A few drinks and dinner maybe," Craig said, raising a single eyebrow. It was a trick he'd practiced in the mirror for years and had proved a useful asset on the rare occasion he was granted a close-up.

"Throw in a movie and you might just seal the deal."

"You ditched me last time we went to the pictures."

"So I owe you another shot," she said.

• • •

They never made it to the movie.

Back at Paula's villa, Craig helped her out of her dress and off of her legs. She was content to leave her dress and underwear on the floor, but she made Craig put her legs away in their case, fitted into their foam holders, so they wouldn't get banged up if things got intense. The task didn't amount to traditional foreplay, but Craig found himself hard just the same, and Paula was likewise aroused and ready. It took no additional coaxing to get him to strip down and mount her on the bed seconds later.

Only one of Paula's legs still had a knee joint. She wrapped it around him, stroking his thigh up and down as he fucked her, kneading one of his buttocks with the calloused nub of her stump. As he got close, she worked a hand down the crack of his ass and stuck a single finger in his anus while she tickled the back of his balls with the tip of her truncated leg. It did the trick, and Craig spasmed inside her for the longest, hardest orgasm he could ever remember having. He was certain he must have burst the condom, but it was safely intact when he withdrew, with a reservoir tip filled to capacity.

"That was quite…something," he said later, once they had both caught their breath and had grown bored of watching the ceiling fan make its lazy revolutions.

"Faint praise," Paula said.

"No," Craig quickly added, "it was great."

"I thought you were into it. You like it kinky."

"I've never been with an amputee before."

"I was referring to the ass play, but whatever floats your boat."

"I'm sorry," Craig said. "I didn't mean to insult you."

"You're not the first guy to think he was pity-fucking the cripple."

"That's not how I meant it at all."

"I know, I'm just messing with your head."

"I've had enough people messing with my head lately. Can't I enjoy a vacation?"

"I'll lay off for a while," Paula promised. "But you're going to have to bang me like that on the regular if you want me to behave myself."

"So it was good for you?"

"Your enthusiasm was in evidence. I appreciate enthusiasm."

•   •   •

Paula's villa was on one of the five fish-shaped islands that were linked together by a causeway. Each island was packed with similar, nearly identical villas. Cookie-cutter luxury is how Craig thought of it, with the only discernable difference between them being the level of excess on display. Most but not all of them had their own swimming pool, with some bigger than others. Paula's pool was a good size, and Craig split his exercise time equally between doing laps and doing Paula. Over the course of the next several days, he barely visited his own hotel room, and eventually moved much of his spare wardrobe to Paula's villa so he could have a change of clothes between workouts.

One day, after a particularly long swim and an exceptionally vigorous fuck, Craig lay spent on the fresh linen. The sheets were changed daily by a cleaning woman who appeared to hold a contract with every second villa on the island and asked no questions about who the strange man suddenly staying with

Paula might be. Craig had done no more than exchange a nod of recognition with the woman, but he was a fan of her work. Everything smelled vaguely of lavender after one of her visits.

"Did you see the Tree of Life?" Paula asked, seemingly at random. Usually she only asked what they should have for dinner, or what bottle of wine they might open next.

"I don't think so," said Craig, like he was really thinking about it. He had no idea what she was talking about.

"How could you miss it?" she said. "The car ride down goes right by it."

It rang a bell as a local attraction, but this conversation was already the most he'd heard about it since he got off the plane.

"Am I supposed to recognize this Tree of Life? It's just a tree, right?"

"It's damn near the only tree in Bahrain."

"I guess I wasn't paying attention."

Paula snuggled close and stroked one of Craig's legs with her thigh.

"Some people think it's the Tree of Life from the Garden of Eden."

"Is that the knowledge of good and evil tree?"

"No, it's the immortality one. Hence the name. We should go see it."

"You mean like a road trip across the country?"

"It's a very small country."

"I don't know," said Craig. "I'm enjoying living in a luxury resort with nothing but oceanfront property as far as the eye can see. Why would I want to head inland? That's where they keep all the desert."

"How else are we going to pass the time?" asked Paula. "It's the wrong season for the Grand Prix or the Jazz Festival."

"I'm enjoying the swimming and the sex," Craig said. "I think it's going to take a long time for that to grow old."

"You can skip a swim for a day trip. As for the other thing, there are places to stay out in the desert."

"I don't know," said Craig. "Do they have villas and luxury hotels inland?"

"There are camp sites all over the place," said Paula, who considered herself an expert after reading no fewer than three hotel pamphlets on the subject. "They're popular in the winter when it's cool enough to enjoy a night out in the desert. Nobody camps in the summer when the heat is brutal. We're between seasons, so it shouldn't be too hot, or too crowded."

● ● ●

The taxi knew just where to take them. The Tree of Life was the only significant landmark as far as the eye could see, situated at the highest point of the island nation. It was the one bit of greenery beyond the patches of parched shrubbery, with a tangle of enormous branches hanging low and wide over the rocky soil. A dirt road ran a wide uneven circle around the site that saw a steady flow of tourists year round. The tree, gnarled and ancient, was not an exceptionally remarkable tree except for the fact that it shouldn't have been there at all. No one knew for sure where it found its nourishment, but the roots, estimated to have burrowed at least fifty meters down, must have found water in some unknown subterranean chamber. The locals had harvested the tree for resin and beans for centuries, with candles and jam made from it fetching a premium price at the nearby markets.

"Impressive, isn't it?" said Paula as they strode towards the living monument from an informal parking lot that served as a drop-off point for visitors.

"It's certainly a big old tree," agreed Craig, who had seen his fair share. Admittedly, none of them in a desert wasteland, and all of them thousands of miles from Bahrain.

"You could almost believe it came right out of the Bible."

Its twisted form and scale was one thing, but it was its surreal isolation that truly evoked the fantastical.

"Is that what you believe?" Craig asked.

"No," replied Paula. "Like most religious artifacts, it's a forgery from the middle ages. This one was planted sometime in the sixteenth century. But it's fun to pretend."

Craig had never spent so much time staring at a single tree before, but there was nothing else of note to see in the area beyond a shelter that offered relief from the sun and the wind. One side of the enclosure presented a view of the tree, the other a series of photographs—also of the tree.

Once they'd had their fill, Craig and Paula checked in at one of the nearby campgrounds. Even out in the desert terrain, the camps hardly qualified as roughing it. They all had fire pits for socializing, and indoor toilets for privacy. A burger joint was a short walk away if the restaurants offering local cuisine did not appeal.

"It's weird, don't you think?" said Paula, as they lay on a couple of blankets staring up at the canopy of stars that had replaced the spectacular sunset.

"What is?" asked Craig, who already thought there were plenty of things in his life competing for weirdest.

"You and me, actors far from home, our careers already over and done with just when we should be hitting our prime."

"I guess it feels weird knowing that I'm never going to act again. Never going to another audition. Never stepping foot on stage or in front of a camera. I thought I'd be doing that for the rest of my life."

"Not many actors get to enjoy that sort of longevity," said Paula. "Usually they just fade away and become has-beens. Or the jobs dry up and they go do something else. Only a select few get to step off the stage in their prime. Like a James Dean or a Jayne Mansfield."

"They died," noted Craig.

"So did we."

"Not for real."

"For real enough."

The universe above seemed so static. Only the occasional shooting star, caught at the periphery of vision, gone in a split second, broke the illusion of stillness. That or the sun reflecting off a satellite, passing across the vista in low Earth orbit, slow enough and bright enough to follow with the naked eye.

"Sometimes I think I'd like to get back in the game. I miss it," said Paula after a protracted silence.

"Maybe there's a way you could reinvent yourself," suggested Craig.

"There are only so many noses you can wear on any one face."

They had a room waiting for them inside, but the swinging temperatures of the desert were kind that evening, and the air had cooled without chilling enough to become uncomfortable. Paula dozed off before the moon had fully risen, but Craig was restless, and there had been more moving specks of light in the sky than he cared to count. After an hour of soft snoring and no more words from Paula, he rose from his blanket and took a slow walk back towards the tree. There was no missing it, even in the middle of the night. Spotlights at the base lit it from a variety of low angles, providing the leaves and bark an eerie underglow against the night sky.

Craig approached, careful not to trip over the stone foundations of various small buildings that used to surround the tree in generations past. He was not alone. There was one other tourist meditating upon The Tree of Life that night. The man sat on the edge of one of the foundations, his feet in the loose dirt that used to be solid floor centuries ago.

"Pull up some ruins and have a seat," Brett Wolcott said to Craig.

"I won't ask how you found me," Craig replied, joining him.

"See? You're getting the hang of this."

"Just in time for my retirement."

"As it turns out, you're not quite as retired as any of us thought you were."

Craig felt a flutter in his chest and couldn't decide if it was excitement or fear. He'd seen the balance in his brand-new bank account. It was a lot. Enough. But he wanted more. Not necessarily money, though he was open to topping off enough with more-than-enough. He wanted one last taste of the crisis limelight. A brief cable-news interview and a single-take slaying in an Arizona warehouse had not been the career capstone he'd envisioned.

"You're being called back for reshoots," Brett specified.

"Reshoots?" Craig asked, bewildered. "Who does reshoots on a snuff film?"

"We need a few more seconds of footage for an extended cut."

A few more seconds didn't amount to a comeback, but it was something. It was, at the very least,

the take two Craig had wanted during principal pho-
tography. He was sure he could dig deep and muster
a better death if given the opportunity.

"I'll go tell Paula I'm leaving," he said.

"No need to tell Peggy anything."

"Her name is Paula."

"She's 'Peggy' to us. As in peg-leg."

"That's a mean thing to call her."

"I'm not calling her anything," said Brett. "It's her
codename."

"Then it's a mean codename."

"Codenames often are."

"Do I have a codename?"

"Of course."

"What is it?"

"You don't want to know."

"Is it mean?"

"It's pretty mean."

"Is it meaner than naming an amputee 'Peggy'?"

Brett offered no further comment.

"I should leave a note," said Craig,

"No notes. We just go."

And just like that, they went.

11

A PRIVATE JET WAS WAITING on Bahrain's strategically significant tarmac. Craig and Brett were the only passengers. There was enough fuel for a direct flight, but Craig was told they'd be making a pit stop in Germany to pick up some additional baggage. He hoped there would be a change of clothes and some toiletries to go with this supply run. Spirited away from the campsite so abruptly, he hadn't even been able to retrieve the modest overnight he'd brought on the excursion with Paula.

They landed at the Ramstein Air Base where the usual bother of customs and security was waived. There was only a cursory inspection of passports. Craig hadn't been permitted to retrieve his, but Brett had a duplicate waiting for him on the plane, complete with duplicate stamps of the few places he'd been. Craig inspected the copy closely during the flight and decided it wasn't a counterfeit but rather a real passport obtained for him from official government sources and then altered by unofficial government sources.

A car was provided and Brett took the driver's seat. In less than fifteen minutes from the moment the wheels of the jet touched down, they were driving through the gate and off the base for a destination Craig had yet to be told.

"Where…?" he began, once they were on the autobahn. Brett let him get no further.

"Frankfurt," he said.

"So I guess that's no longer a need-to-know state secret."

"You can read road signs," said Brett. "You would have figured it out."

"Where are we going in Frankfurt?" asked Craig, who had never been to Frankfurt before. Nor Germany. Nor Europe in general, barring his recent connecting flight and two-hour stopover.

"Probably some fucking golf course."

"You don't like golf?"

"I don't like the sort of fucks who play golf," said Brett.

Sure enough, the swanky hotel they pulled up to directed them to the adjoining world-class eighteen holes. Craig hadn't heard who Brett asked after, but by the time they arrived at the clubhouse he knew. The whole place was thick with portly rich men who looked like CEOs, CFOs, and those elected to high office. He instinctively looked for the one he was personally acquainted with but couldn't spot him.

A caddie approached Brett like he knew exactly who he was. He probably did. Well-informed and attentive caddies made the best tips, and the high rollers thought nothing of dropping four figures on one who could advise them well on the green and anticipate their needs back at the bar.

"The senator is driving a few on the range," came the report.

Brett was not forthcoming with financial compensation for the insight. Without a word of thanks, he led Craig out to a platform overlooking a scenic fairway that would have been a uniformly green landscape if not for the thousand white balls littering the field, and the caged yellow tractor driving back and forth to scoop them up in its undercarriage retrieval mechanism.

Senator Wolcott was working up a sweat, improving his form if not his aim, as he swatted another dimpled golf ball into the distance with a wooden driver. The range was nearly vacant, with all the other golfers eager to make the most of a nice day and get a proper game in, rather than pass the time trying to hit the distant tractor and make its pilot jump.

"Senator," said Brett coldly to his father, announcing their arrival.

"Look at you two! Look at you two!" Wolcott said genially when he saw Craig in the company of his son. "It's a pleasure to see you boys getting along so famously. Brett always did have trouble making new friends."

"We're not friends," Brett clarified.

"Your timing is perfect," said the senator, ignoring his son's poor attitude. "Just the excuse I need to slip away before the meetings get underway in earnest."

"I wouldn't want to interrupt any important work you have on your plate," Craig said.

"Not at all! You're rescuing me from a slow death by boredom. A bunch of self-styled autocrats trying to agree on the fate of the world—not that it ever pans out as intended."

"Wait, is this the Bilderberg Group I keep hearing about?"

Craig looked around, half expecting to spot Felix Hinch waving a banner at the head of a protest group.

"Don't be silly," said Senator Wolcott. "The Bilderbergers are passé. Everyone's heard of them now, so what's the point of a secret meeting of the elite if we can't be secretive about it? No, Bilderberg has turned into a golf vacation for the rich and powerful."

"So what do you call this, then?" asked Brett, grabbing a driver off a rack full of them and taking a mock swing at an imaginary ball.

"This is the golf vacation where we talk shop on the greens. Meat and potatoes stuff. All you hear at Bilderberg these days is a lot of stock tips and insider trading, which has to get tedious once you already have more money than God."

The senator took Craig aside and spoke in a low voice.

"I do not have more money than God. Which is why I still drop by Bilderberg when I can."

He winked at Craig, as though he had just confided a secret. He hadn't. Brett was within earshot and well aware of the state of the family fortune: substantial, but sub-deity.

• • •

They were back in the car to complete the round trip to the airbase before Craig felt he'd even had a chance to stretch his legs. Senator Wolcott was wrapping up his most pressing bit of outstanding business, even as he abandoned the golf greens for greener pastures.

"Tell Henry he'll just need to find someone else to fill the foursome."

He disconnected and put away the phone.

"Poor old bastard is too old to swing a club, but he likes to watch and get some sun. He lets his partner tee off for him, but he'll still make a putt now and then if he's well positioned."

Only once they were on the jet, its engine still warm from the first leg of its itinerary, and taxiing down the runway, did Wolcott mention the emergency reshoots that had necessitated Craig being recalled. The reaction to Craig's execution had not been all that had been hoped for. Comment sections and

4chan groups were flooded with film critics and skeptics, and it was not dying down quick enough. Mainstream media penetration was all but ensured if it continued.

The senator explained, "We staged a bloodless beheading in front of a green screen and got called on it. The video crew was so involved trying to fine tune the background and the lighting so we could have a convincing desert exterior in-studio, nobody seemed to notice the lack of red as the jihadist starts sawing away at the hostage's neck with the dummy knife. Not that the networks we were feeding were ever going to show an arterial money shot, but the footage we gave them went on for about two seconds too long. Just long enough for the picky people who saw it to start asking, 'Where's the blood?' It was really a fault in the editing. Up to that point, it was perfectly convincing. Social media lit up. I think the real problem is that there are too many videos of actual decapitations online. Between the drug cartels and guerrilla freedom fighters and the goddamn Saudi government, it's too easy for curious civilians to go see what a beheading looks like. So when you give them a fake, even with all the production value money can buy, they call bullshit on it. Of course we have our own crackpots on the payroll to refute them, denounce them as alt-right trolls, and generally muddy the waters. But that doesn't excuse sloppy work."

The plan was to make a hard-R cut of the closing moments of the video. A hint of a gore effect, strategically leaked after the fact to the darker corners of the web, would be discovered by the most ghoulish of surfers, and word of the "uncensored" footage would spread from there. The skeptics would forever remain skeptical, but doubt would take root in the conspiracy community and they would, in time, move on. A potential new disinformation campaign to expose was only ever one or two days away.

"I suggested we just CGI it," said the senator, "but Brett seems to think it always looks fake."

"CGI is shit," said Brett.

"Stage blood obeys the laws of physics," agreed Craig. "They still can't quite get that right on a computer."

"I'm told the tech nerds will only end up going through the new footage frame by frame, looking for post-production tampering," Wolcott said. "No use giving them more ammunition. I'll defer to the experts. You've seen enough blood spilled on the stage, my boy. And Brett has made enough of the real stuff flow."

The flight was smooth and the winds favourable. A fine wine was served, and it made napping to pass the time easier.

"I never thought I'd come back here again," Craig commented, when he recognized where they were landing eight hours later.

"We held onto our local assets, fortunately," said Senator Wolcott of the desolate little Arizona town. "Luckily property values are in the toilet and nobody was beating down the door to rent out our studio from under us."

The airfield was a privately owned strip of dirt with a wind sock and no frills. A car was waiting with the keys in the ignition. No one was around to greet them or steal the car.

"Grab a bite," Wolcott said, once they drove into town and let Craig out in front of the local diner. "Brett and I are going to make sure everything is good to go on set. You remember the way?"

Craig did. Even if he didn't, the town was too small to miss the converted warehouse where he'd so recently lost his head the first time.

The diner was strictly greasy-spoon, but served a decent all-day breakfast. Craig ordered himself toast, eggs, and coffee with all the sides included in the Hungry Man special. He was no more than two sips and three bites in before another familiar face walked through the door.

"Maziar!" he called out, and waved his co-star over.

"My man!" Maziar said, exchanging a knuckle-bumping, palm-slapping handshake that Craig only got half right. "You're looking well for a dead man."

"I just hope I didn't tan enough to screw up continuity."

"What's edible?" Maziar asked, sitting down in the booth across from Craig and flipping through a menu.

"The bacon is good," suggested Craig.

"I'm half Jewish, half Muslim, so I'm doubly out on the bacon."

He opted for black coffee and plain toast when the waitress came around.

"I was on the other side of the world when they pulled me out for round two," he told Maziar once his food was served. "I thought I was all-the-way retired."

"They'll always get you with the contractual reshoots," Maziar said. "I was doing second-unit on a spy thriller outside Edinburgh when I got the call. Took the red eye to get here in time. You'd think they'd figure out their shot list before they send everyone home, but no. There's always one more angle they want to get after the fact."

"I hear our little snuff film didn't test so well."

"You can't please everybody," said Maziar. "On my other gig, some studio executive decided the action hero should kill me with a flame thrower instead of a nail gun. A stunt man did most of it. All they wanted out of me was a different face for the close-up. Like my character was going to have a profoundly different reaction getting murdered one way over another."

"You were playing another bad guy?"

"Terrorist," Maziar shrugged. "Typecast again."

"You must find that insulting as an Arab," Craig said.

"I don't."

"No?"

"I'm not an Arab. I'm Persian. I find it insulting as a Persian."

"I don't know the difference," Craig admitted.

"Arabs and Persians do," said Maziar. "Nobody else really gives a shit."

"Maybe I do. Give me an example."

"Okay, for instance, broadly speaking, Persians are the ones who like to shout 'Death to America.' Arabs are the ones who actually kill Americans."

"That seems like a subtle distinction."

"You'd understand it better if you were Persian. Or an Arab."

"Did you ever chant 'Death to America' growing up in Iran?"

"Oh sure. All the time. Don't take it personally. It doesn't really mean much."

"It kinda sounds like you want America to die."

"It's a Persian thing. We're always wishing death on someone. You, me, America. Everything. Most of our common expressions are about death. If you want a more faithful translation into English, replace every instance of 'death to' with 'fuck.' Then you'll understand."

Craig thought about it, and repeated back the sentiment.

"Fuck me, fuck you, fuck America..."

"Fuck everything," agreed Maziar.

"I think I get it," Craig nodded.

"And do you agree?"

"Some days."

"There you go. One step closer to understanding Persians."

"Thanks. That was helpful."

"Building bridges, man. Building bridges."

"You think we'll be done here soon enough for you to get back to your other reshoots?" Craig asked.

"I should be finished there," replied Maziar. "I gave them about fifty different takes of my best death throes. If they can't cut something together for however they decide to kill me, there's nothing else I can do for them. But yeah, I wouldn't mind getting the hell out of here sooner rather than later. I'm up for a romantic lead, and I wouldn't want to turn it down over some stupid scheduling conflict."

"Hey, good for you!" said Craig, pleased to be the first to congratulate Maziar. "Things are looking up. Is it a rom com?"

"Well, no," admitted Maziar. "It's more of a sexual-abuse melodrama. I take a girl hostage and threaten to kill her."

"Where's the romantic-lead part come in?"

"She gets Stockholm syndrome."

"Well, that's something," Craig said. "At least it's a step in the right direction and you're not playing a foreign terrorist."

"Domestic terrorist," shrugged Maziar.

He had nibbled on his toast but had been neglecting his beverage. Maziar took a sip and made a face.

Not a happy one. The brew was a thin broth that tasted like mop water.

"Death to this coffee," he said.

• • •

Twenty minutes later, their diner bill paid, Craig and Maziar entered the studio and reported for duty. Brett was there, watching the door for their arrival.

"Mr. Gholami," Brett said, waving Maziar over. "A word."

"Have a good shoot," Maziar told Craig as they parted ways. They would be in character the next time they saw each other and would likely not be able to engage in further casual conversation.

"You too," Craig said, and submitted himself to the costume and makeup departments.

The jumpsuit might have been the exact one he'd been ill-fitted for last time, but the natural dishevelled look needed to be faithfully recreated in decidedly unnatural ways. Craig spent two hours in the chair getting his hair precisely teased to look perfectly un-kempt, while layers of primer and foundation were laid down so he could be made to look as pale and neglected as he had for the original shoot.

When Craig was finally led to the set, he found the squad of black-clad terrorists waiting for him. It was hard to say if Maziar's backup chorus was the same group of men as before. He'd never had the chance to become acquainted with any of them.

"There's our star!" announced Senator Wolcott upon seeing Craig in costume. "What an encore this shall be!"

"Hey, Maziar," Craig waved at the lead terrorist.

He assumed it was Maziar behind the mask, based on the mark he was positioned upon. Maziar did not wave back. Instead, he seemed to be muttering to himself, eyes down, as he prepared for the scene. Praying would have been Craig's guess. He left his fellow actor alone with his method, regardless of whether or not it was The Method, and waited to receive direction from Wolcott.

"We're playing this one a little more loose," the senator informed him, "from a whole other angle. The idea is to suggest there was someone else present at the execution, recording it on their phone. Everything will match up just like people who saw the first video remembers. Except this time there will be a few added seconds of nastiness that should convince them that the earlier release was cut off before things got too ugly."

"Sure thing," Craig agreed, no stranger to gore effects.

"If you'll just take your position. Same as before."

The fake desert sand had been replenished and brushed into a carefully sculpted dune that was a reasonable match for the last one Craig had been beheaded on. He planted his knees into a mark of his own, one step in front of Maziar, and presented his neck accordingly.

Maziar gently placed his hand on Craig's head, running his fingers tenderly through his hair, before seizing a firm handhold and positioning his giant knife within an inch of his throat.

"Hey, man," said Craig, tilting his head back and smiling at his executioner, "no jokes this time?"

"No," he croaked, "no jokes."

The sunlamps came on, blinding Craig, but he could see the Wolcotts past the haze, positioned a single pace beyond the equipment that was assembled to capture the recreated moment.

"Everyone knows what to do?" Brett asked of the crew.

There were various reports of "check" from the different technical stations, but Brett seemed particularly keen to hear from Maziar. He stared at the actor intensely, waiting for his confirmation.

"Yes, sir," said Maziar, in a low voice that was barely more than a loud whisper.

"Same as before," instructed Senator Wolcott, "but, you know, with a little extra energy, right?"

"Right," Maziar echoed back.

Someone from the crew brought the senator a bundle of plastic wrap, neatly folded. Wolcott accepted the delivery and shook the cover out before pulling it on and smoothing it down over his clothes. The clear slicker sported a hood at the back, which he drew over his head.

"What's that for?" Craig asked.

"Protection," said the senator.

"From what?"

"Humidity. It's a very expensive suit."

Craig hadn't seen the weather forecast, but the walk from the diner had felt like an arid heat to him.

"And the rubber boots?" Craig queried of the twin galoshes the big man subsequently stepped into.

"Wouldn't want to get my Italian loafers wet either."

"This is just a rehearsal, right?" Craig asked, knowing it had to be. No one had run any tubes up his jump suit yet, or taped any nozzles to his neck so arterial spray could be convincingly simulated.

"Call it a dry run," said the senator, and gestured to the camera operator. The recording commenced.

"You're rolling?" Craig asked.

"Making sure everything is in good working order," the senator winked at him.

Maziar held the knife at Craig's throat. It was in exactly the same location, at the same angle, as it had been last time. The two takes would line up perfectly. But something was different. Maziar's hand was trembling. The tremor became so pronounced, he nicked Craig just below his beard line. Craig had done worse shaving, but felt blood had likely been drawn.

"Watch it, Maziar," Craig cautioned him. "That thing's fucking sharp. Where's the prop knife?"

"Action!" Brett bellowed, which made Maziar jump slightly. He gripped Crag's hair hard enough to pull a few strands out by the roots.

"What do mean, 'Action'?" said Craig. "I haven't been outfitted with a squib yet."

"Action," Brett reiterated, directing Maziar and Maziar alone.

But Maziar froze, unable to act. It was like he had suddenly developed a paralytic case of state fright. When, at last, he moved, it was only his lips.

"Run," Maziar whispered.

"Run?" Craig asked.

"Run!" his co-star shouted.

"That's not your line."

Craig wondered if there was a new draft of the script he hadn't seen.

Brett was the first to step forward once it was clear the scene was not going to play out as planned. A few other crew members joined him, prepared to help bring the situation under control and get the day's shoot done one way or another.

Maziar threw the knife at the advancing men. It was a terrible throw, missed everybody, and bounced off the camera after it struck the tripod hilt-first. But it was enough to make everybody duck for a moment. He turned to flee and found a wall of black silk robes in his path. The chorus of backup terrorists did not try to detain him, but they were blocking the way just the same. One of them stepped forward and laid his hands on Maziar's shoulders, making eye contact and attempting to calm him down.

"You got this," he was told. "You got this."

Maziar threw a punch. It wasn't a good punch, and hit his jihadist lieutenant in the forehead—not hard enough to knock him down, but hard enough to make him wince.

"Ow! You bloody tit!" the man behind the mask exclaimed in a thick cockney accent.

"I'm sorry!" Maziar told him, and seized the opportunity to run around him while he was still stunned by the blow.

"Maziar! Where are you going?" Craig called after him, scrambling to his feet on the loose sand base and kicking the grit out of his sandals.

Craig threw up his hands, warning off the crew and extras as they closed in.

"Don't worry," he assured them all, "I'll talk to him."

He raced after Maziar, following him around the side of the giant backdrop and finding him pushing through a fire exit behind the green screen.

"Wait!" Craig shouted at him.

Maziar paused in the open doorway, briefly considering his options, and then grabbed Craig by the arm and pulled him through. A moment later they found themselves out in the blinding Arizona sun— hotter and brighter than the artificial dessert sun inside the sound stage.

"Come on!" Maziar encouraged, giving Craig a shove forward before outpacing him at a full sprint.

Craig gave chase but likely would have fallen far behind if Maziar didn't keep looking back over his shoulder at the nondescript studio bunker and the gaping dark door that was slowly swinging shut again.

No one was coming after them.

"They're not chasing us," Maziar observed, slowing his pace to a steady jog.

"Who's going to run after us?" Craig asked, winded. "A fat politician and a bunch of non-speaking-part extras?"

"They won't let us go so easy!"

"Who's going? You're just having a bit of a freak out. Let's take a break, do some breathing exercises, and go back to finish the scene."

"There's no going back!" Maziar insisted. "Not for me and definitely not for you!"

"Of course I'm going back," said Craig. "I mean, I'm not under contract. Not officially. But I have a role to play."

Maziar stood in place and Craig was glad to stop chasing him.

"Don't you get it? They told me to kill you! To cut your throat ear to ear."

"That's the scene."

"For real this time!"

"They wanted me dead?" said Craig, letting it sink in.

"They don't want you dead," Maziar clarified. "They just want you to die."

"But we could have faked it."

"Not as good as the real thing," said Maziar. "The most convincing special effect is no special effect at all."

They were nearly a quarter of a mile out from the studio and there was still no hint of anyone pursuing them.

"I don't see anyone," observed Craig. "No one at all."

"They're coming for us just the same," said Maziar. "They can't let us walk away. Not now. Not knowing what we know."

"What we know?" Craig protested. "I don't know anything! Least of all what's going on."

"We were part of a major false-flag operation," Maziar explained. "Now we're part of a major cover-up. And there's a lot of desert out here for them to cover us both up."

"We should go, then," agreed Craig, after as much consideration as he dared spend time on. "Get a ride out of the town. Disappear. Leave no trace."

"We can't escape them. They'll find us. They're the government!"

"One senator."

"Acting on whose behalf? How high up does this go? Who authorized this?"

Craig had to admit he didn't understand how deep the plot ran, or how far they would go to conceal it now that two of their crisis actors were off script.

"What's the plan?" he asked.

"Plan? I have no plan!" Maziar yelled, panic rising. "Everything went to shit five minutes ago! That's not long enough to come up with a plan!"

"We need to get away from here. Keep our heads down and figure out who to tell to expose this whole fraud."

"Where can we go? Where can we hide? Who would even believe us?"

Craig already knew the answer to all of those questions.

12

THEY TOOK THE SECOND BUS out of town, paying cash for two tickets one-way. Maziar was worried all their obvious moves would be anticipated, and that the bus station would be the first avenue of escape that would be checked. The inevitable search party would assume they grabbed the next available Greyhound, so that's why he suggested they lay low and board the one after that, half an hour later. It didn't matter where it was going, so long as it was away from the snuff film they had been cast in as victim and victimizer.

As they hid in two adjacent bathroom stalls, the doors latched shut and their feet perched atop the toilet lids, Craig and Maziar waited the excruciating extra minutes for their departure to be announced.

"You need to lose the prisoner jumper," Maziar whispered to the neighbouring stall. "You look like you just escaped from a supermax."

They had both retained their wallets, tucked away in their costumes, knowing that there were always sticky fingers on any film set. When they pooled their cash, Maziar went and bought the tickets that would take them as far as the nearest major city. From there they could choose a target destination that wasn't so randomly determined by short time and desperation.

"What about you?" Craig asked him.

"What about me?"

"You look like Omar Sharif threw a star-fit and walked off the set of *Lawrence of Arabia*."

"It'll turn fewer heads than your prison orange."

"It's all I'm wearing."

"Don't tell me you're naked under that thing."

"I've got underwear and a t-shirt on," said Craig, declaring his complete wardrobe.

"Tighty-whities?"

"Boxers."

"That's practically formal wear on a Greyhound."

"I can't ride across state lines in my underwear."

"If you're shy about it, we'll find someone your size once we're onboard and buy their shirt and jeans."

"What random person is going to sell me the shirt off their back?"

"Someone who wants twenty dollars more than a five-dollar shirt."

• • •

No one tried to stop them when they boarded the bus to Tucson—not for fleeing the scene of a grand government conspiracy, nor for violating transit dress codes.

A second bus got them as far as Phoenix, and from there they had just enough cash left to get on a long-haul that would take them back east to the one place Craig hoped they could find safe harbour.

It was past midnight the next day when Craig leaned on the call button for a fourth-floor apartment in a dumpy end of the city he used to call home. The rude hour was compounded by the visit being unannounced and likely unwelcome.

"Are you sure he's home?" Maziar asked when they weren't buzzed in and no voice came over the speaker to see who was ringing.

"He's got nowhere better to be," said Craig.

"Maybe he's a heavy sleeper."

"Maybe. But I'm betting he's the type who's up all night and sleeps all afternoon."

There was no camera trained on the door, but Craig felt like they were being watched just the same. He stepped off the front stoop of the building and looked up. Poised on one of the balconies several floors up was a man in a bathrobe staring down at them. There was a dim light on in the apartment behind him. Judging from the flickering, it was either a television or a computer monitor.

"Felix?" Craig called up to him.

"Who the hell is it?" came the answer back down.

"It's Craig Linton."

"Who's he?" Felix asked of Maziar.

"A friend," was all Craig could explain without launching into a long explanation in the middle of the street.

"What are you doing here? Did the Illuminati kick you out?" Felix sneered.

"Yes."

Felix Hinch did not have a sarcastic response ready for that.

"Want to hear the inside scoop?" Craig asked.

Felix turned his back on them and disappeared into his apartment, shutting the balcony door behind him. Craig thought his pitch might have failed, but no more than ten seconds later the door buzzer sounded, unlocking the mechanism and allowing them access to the lobby.

● ● ●

"How did you find me?" Felix asked, once the two men got off the elevator and arrived at his door.

"You gave me your card," said Craig, holding up the slip of rigid paper that had been in his wallet since the night they first met.

"That's my business card," Felix said.

"I thought it had a certain home-office vibe to it."

"You said this place was off the grid," Maziar reminded Craig.

"It's off-the-grid lite," said Felix defensively. "I haven't gone full-prepper mode just yet. Give me another year or two and I'll have saved up enough for a nice little bunker out in the woods."

"You going to invite us in?" Craig asked.

"I haven't decided yet," was the non-committal reply.

"You think it's safe for us to talk out in the hall?"

It baited Felix as Craig knew it would. He let his apartment door swing wide. Once they were in, he triple-bolted it and locked a security bar in place for good measure.

"I hope we aren't interrupting anything," Craig said.

"Just some online *Call of Duty*," said Felix. "Typical Friday night. So tell me why you're not hanging out with your elitist pals, and are back here slumming it with a fringe nutjob instead."

"Turns out you were right about everything," said Craig.

"Of course I was right!" declared Felix, adding, "Which specific part was I right about? I have a lot of controversial opinions."

"They're all out to get us," Maziar summarized.

"Now you know how I feel," said Felix.

• • •

It only took Craig twenty minutes to spell out what the last two weeks of his life had been like. Felix fell silent for the duration—probably the longest he'd ever held his tongue in a conversation. Maziar added a few details from his end of things, but it was Craig, as a lead player, who had the most harrowing tale to tell. Mostly Maziar was there to back up as many unbelievable assertions as he could.

"I know it sounds like a crazy conspiracy theory…" Maziar apologized, as Craig brought Felix up to date to the moment he rang his doorbell.

"They're all conspiracy theories right up until they become historical fact," Felix assured him. "Operation Paperclip, Project Sunshine, The Gulf of Tonkin, MK-ULTRA. Why should this one be any different?"

"I don't know what any of those things are," confessed Craig.

"You should," said Felix. "Here's another conspiracy theory for you: the term 'conspiracy theory' was concocted by the CIA in order to discredit anybody who asked questions about the JFK assassination."

"Yeah, that sounds like a conspiracy theory all right," Craig agreed.

"Everybody believes in conspiracies," said Felix. "Everybody."

"I never used to," Craig mused. "I guess now I do—mostly because I'm involved in one. But I know people who don't."

"Do they believe in 9/11?"

"Probably not many of them."

"I don't mean the stories surrounding 9/11," Felix specified, "I mean the event itself."

"Sure. We all saw it on TV."

"Not like TV ever lies," added Maziar.

"I've been to New York," said Craig. "Millions have. We saw the holes in the ground."

"So we all agree it happened," Felix confirmed.

"Sure," Craig shrugged.

"Then we're all conspiracy theorists now. It's just a matter of which conspiracy you believe in. Either you think it was nineteen hijackers colluding to crash planes into buildings, or you think it was an inside job committed by shadowy government forces intent on pushing an agenda. Either way, it was a conspiracy."

"I'm sure I don't need to ask which version you believe in," said Craig.

"There's a lot of information to dig through, but let me make it real simple for you," said Felix. "Number of times a steel-frame skyscraper collapsed prior to 9/11? Zero. Number of steel-frame skyscrapers that collapsed on 9/11? Three. Number of steel-frame skyscrapers that collapsed since 9/11? Zero."

"What was the third skyscraper to collapse on 9/11?" Craig asked.

"Are you serious?"

"Building Seven, dumbass," Maziar interjected. "I was a child thousands of miles away and I know that."

It rang a bell. Just a small one. It tinkled slightly.

"Building Seven wasn't hit by any airplane," recalled Craig.

"Exactly," said Felix.

He opened another can of soda and sucked the foam off the top so he could better access his next hit of sugar and caffeine.

"You think I want to believe the things I believe?" he said after his next swallow. "I don't. The world would be a much simpler place if I could buy into any of the official narratives. The state-approved stories. But I have to go where the facts take me, and they take me to dark places I don't like."

Maziar nodded knowingly.

"You can lead a blind man to water. You can even dunk his head in the lake. But you can't make him see it."

Felix raised his can in solidarity and downed the rest.

"What you know would make some men nervous, my friend," said Maziar.

"I have my bugout bag for the day they figure out I'm onto them and they come after me."

"If you're so paranoid about it, why do you keep talking about it so openly?" asked Craig.

"I have a big mouth," Felix admitted.

"Try shutting it."

"You're just pissed that I'm right all the time."

Maziar ignored the exchange. He had become distracted by a hint of movement outside the living-room window.

"There's someone on your fire escape," he informed Felix.

"There's no fire escape there," Felix said.

But when they looked, they could all see the shape of a man right behind the glass. He wasn't standing on a ledge or a fire escape. He was dangling from a rope he had used to repel down the side of the building from the roof.

Just then, there was a tremendous thud against the door, like someone had tried to kick it in and failed. The security bar had held strong.

"Ow," said a voice behind the door. Probably the owner of the foot.

"Hit squad!" Maziar concluded in a panic.

"They found us!" Craig cried out. "Somehow they found us!"

"They're not here for you," Felix said, consulting the chat window on his computer. "They're here for me."

"What the hell did you do, Felix?"

"Nothing," said Felix, manning his keyboard. "It's that bastard, Jarbo69. The little shit swatted me!"

"Who's Jarbo69?"

"Some *Call of Duty* anklebiter I play with. He doesn't like it when I teabag him every time he gets fragged."

Felix furiously typed a brief message and hit return. At a glance, Craig could see it was instructing Jarbo69 exactly how and where he should sexually violate his mother.

Having spent a few vital seconds on a parting insult, Felix wasted no more time.

"Come on!" he demanded of his house guests, leading them to the bedroom.

The SWAT team was trying the door again. This time with a battering ram. The security bar withstood the next two blows, but a third was not guaranteed. Meanwhile, the dangling member of the team pushed off hard to give himself the most distance and speed to swing with. Felix had barely enough time to slam the bedroom door shut behind them before the window imploded and let the first invader in. A couple of seconds later they heard the security bar snap off its mooring and clatter across the floor. No doubt the team was already assembling and training their rifles on the door the suspects had vanished behind.

"This way," Felix instructed, like he was well practised for such a contingency.

He was holding another door open for his guests. Craig and Maziar didn't question Felix's escape route and hustled through, only to find themselves up against a wall a moment later. Felix entered the space with them, shut the door, and turned on the overhead light with a pull chain. He had led them into a closet, barely big enough to contain all three men.

"Clear!" came a commanding shout from the living room as the SWAT team confirmed that that room, at least, contained no hostiles. Two more reports of "Clear!" suggested they were equally satisfied with the state of the kitchen and the bathroom. That only left the one bedroom.

"This way," said Felix, ducking down and pulling an access panel off the wall just above the baseboard.

A crawlspace exposed the building's water main in the event of a leak that required a plumber get to the pipes without demolishing walls. There was enough room for a grown man to squeeze in, wriggle around and, if necessary, wield a wrench. Felix wormed his way through until his feet vanished into the dark hole. Maziar was quick to follow, more willing to face the likelihood of spider webs and asbestos dust than then rifles of militarized police.

Whatever space existed beyond the entry point was able to accommodate two, so Craig committed to seeing if it could fit a third. He shut off the closet light, got down on all fours, and backed into the hole so he could set the panel cover in place once he was inside. No sooner had he hooked it back on the loose nails in the wall than he heard the bedroom door implode. The men sweeping the room would have the closet door open in moments, so Craig backed away as silently as he could, keeping an eye on the panel he had replaced, expecting it to be discovered and peeled aside at any moment.

It remained shut. Craig kept backing away regardless, waiting to bump up against Maziar behind him once he ran out of room, but the passage remained open. Eventually Craig backed into a new light source and found himself in a whole other closet. Unlike Felix's barren little wardrobe, this one was stuffed full of clothes. Most of it, Craig realized once his eyes adjusted, was lingerie.

The closet door hung open and the bedroom beyond was illuminated with an array of semi-professional stage lighting that would have broken the budget of many an independent film studio. The camera and computer equipment similarly skirted the edge of being high-end indie or low-end Hollywood.

The star of the production was there to greet the interlopers, but she didn't seem pleased by their arrival.

"Oh, hello," Craig said to the woman in garters and little else.

There was enough exposed flesh to make a reasonably accurate count of her tattoos. She was dressed for bed, but not for sleeping. Craig thought they must be interrupting a romantic liaison, but she had been alone in the room before three adult males came spilling out of her closet.

"Jesus Christ, Felix," she said, "how many more are there?"

"That's everybody," Felix assured her.

"I hope you're not in the middle of anything," Craig apologized.

"Just my regular show for subscribers," she said.

"This is my next-door neighbour, Tiffany," said Felix, adding, "not her real name."

"Not my real tits either, but that's show business."

"Sorry to intrude like this," said Maziar. "We were just following Mr. Hinch here."

"Don't sweat it," said Tiffany, reaching for a robe and pulling it on. "A deal's a deal."

"We have an understanding," Felix explained. "It's a shared escape hatch. I get to use it if The Man ever kicks in my door. Tiffany uses it if one of her fans turns stalker and gets in the building."

"It's happened a few times before," she conceded.

"This is my first time getting swatted, but it was only a matter of time."

"It had to happen during my stream?" Tiffany complained. "I've got a thousand-plus viewers live right now."

"I didn't get a say on the timing," said Felix. "You have it?"

Tiffany sighed and turned to reach under her four-poster bed. Craig couldn't help but notice the variety of oils and adult toys strewn across the mattress. She came up a moment later with a plain gym bag and handed it to Felix.

"One bugout bag," she announced.

"You're a doll," Felix informed her, and unzipped the bag so he could audit the contents.

"You might not want to stand in front of the webcam," Tiffany cautioned Craig and Maziar as they watched the flow of fan feedback rocket across the computer screen.

The speakers rang constantly with bells and whistles warning of incoming tips and superchats. The text was flying by too quickly, but the paid pinned comments were all making obscene requests that involved Tiffany and the two men who had suddenly appeared on her stream. The suggested combinations were inventive and shockingly specific.

"Guys," Tiffany told her audience, addressing the camera, "you know I'm a solo act. These gentlemen are just passing through."

"Could you mute us for a second?" Craig asked Tiffany.

A mouse click shut off the microphone plugged into the computer and Craig was free to ask Felix, "Where are we passing through to?"

"I've got a change of clothes, cash, and fake ID for one," said Felix of his bugout-bag inventory. "It's enough to buy me some distance while the cops figure out I didn't do whatever it was Jarbo69 told them I did. Sorry I couldn't offer you shelter for more than half an hour, but that's life on the run, I guess."

"Wait, that's it?" Maziar asked. "You're ditching us?"

"I don't have some safe house I can spirit you away to," Felix said. "I'm a prepper on a budget. I don't even have a panic room. I have a cheap apartment with a panic closet."

"Guys, I'm on the clock and my views are dropping," Tiffany reminded them.

"We better go," said Felix. "They'll start a door-to-door sweep of the building soon and we want to be gone before that happens."

"I'll show you out," said Tiffany, tying her robe around her waist and sticking her feet in a pair of furry pink slippers.

"You don't have to do that," Craig told her.

"Yeah, I do," she said. "I want to make sure you get away so the cops don't trace you back to my apartment."

Tiffany put a be-right-back banner up on her web page and ran a trailer advertising her many photos and videos for sale.

Sneaking out of the building wasn't as perilous as Craig anticipated it might be. The SWAT team was so focused on the one targeted apartment, they hadn't expanded their operation to secure all possible exits and stairwells yet. Other tenants were in the hall, investigating what the noise was, and served to confuse matters when four people, three of which didn't match the suspect's description, slipped through an emergency exit. A series of interconnected alleys wound their way behind the block of residential low-rents and let them out on an avenue well removed from the scene of the tactical police action.

"This is where we part ways, fellas," Felix told Craig and Maziar.

"Well, it was enlightening as always, Felix," Craig told him.

Tiffany stood watch during the goodbyes, but there was no traffic, pedestrian or car, on the side street they had arrived at. A distant siren could be heard blocks away, but was probably unrelated to the current operation they were fleeing.

"Wrap up it, guys," said Tiffany. "I'm not dressed for cold or public decency."

Rather than disappear into the night straight away, Felix burned an extra few moments looking guilty and uncertain. After some internal debate, Felix dug into his bag and came up with a roll of cash held together with a rubber band. It was a collection of twenties, probably amounting to several hundred dollars. He held it out to Craig.

"Take it," he said. "I'm not so hot that I can't hit a bank machine once I'm out of town. My troubles with the authorities should be sorted out in the next forty-eight hours max. You two sound like you're in a much deeper pile of shit."

Craig accepted the loan, knowing he'd probably never see Felix again to pay it back.

"Wherever you go, whatever you do, pay cash only," advised Felix. "Don't hit an ATM, don't put anything on a credit card. They'll set a new record for response time the moment you stick your heads up, so stay as low to the ground as you can."

"We can't be fugitives for the rest of our lives," Maziar said. "We have to stop running sometime."

"You'll stop once they get the crosshairs of a scoped rifle trained on your head, that's for sure. And then you won't have to worry about the rest of your lives."

"We could go to the media," suggested Craig. "Tell them everything."

"You mean the propaganda wing of the agencies out looking for you right now? Great idea. If you're going to feed yourself to a bear, you might as well cover yourself in barbeque sauce first."

"I'm still learning the ropes of being a fugitive," said Craig.

"It's a hell of a learning curve, I'll give you that," said Felix. "I've been getting ready to disappear without a trace for years. It's a long, involved process. You have maybe a few more hours to figure it out. Being constantly on the move since Arizona is probably the only reason you're still alive. Come morning, somebody's going to spot you. You'll trip up somehow. Count on it. So whatever it is you've got to do, get it done. Wherever it is you think you can hide, get there now. And when they find you—because they will—for fuck's sake don't let them take you alive. Because if they do, they're going to make you tell them everything. Including that I helped you."

"Your name will never come up. Promise," Craig swore.

Again Felix delayed his departure. This time he looked guilty and certain. He reached forward and relieved Craig of the wad of cash he had just gifted him.

"Yeah, they're going to make you tell them everything. I better disappear all the way."

"And…we're broke," Maziar observed. Their cash reserves were officially down to zero, even rounding the number up.

"We'll figure it out," Craig assured Maziar. "Thanks for everything, Felix."

Felix nodded solemnly.

"Thanks for confirming my worst fears."

It sounded like genuine gratitude.

Felix hurried away towards a cross street that would lead him to the next leg of his long-standing escape plan. Tiffany headed in the opposite direction, returning to her apartment and her fans. Before she rounded the corner, she called back to Craig and Maziar.

"If you do go to the media to make a stink and it all turns into some big scandal, be sure you mention my OnlyFans page."

She was gone before they had to make any promises.

13

MORNING CAME AND, just as Felix predicted, Craig and Maziar got spotted. By their estimate, they were spotted by several thousand people before morning rush hour was over. Their intention was to draw the attention of thousands more by early afternoon.

Hiding in plain sight was, they both agreed, a dumb idea, but a necessary one. With no more than a few coins of pocket change between them, they needed seed money to keep running. To that end, they decided to set up shop in a heavily commuted city park, across from a busy subway station, and rely on their unique skill set to see them back to solvency.

Setting down a relatively unsullied pizza box they dug out of the trash, it served to collect donations from nine-to-fivers on their way to the office. In exchange for their micro patronage of the arts, they were fleetingly entertained by Williams and Miller,

Shaw and O'Neill. Anything Craig or Maziar could remember from theatre workshops, acting classes, or past performances was fair game. Collectively they were able to cobble together a selection of notorious scenes from memory, improvising between famous-line landmarks when necessary to bridge half-remembered material.

No one noticed the edits, and few lingered long enough to hear the pair of buskers deliver more than half a monologue, or a fraction of even the most rousing back-and-forth banter. Inevitably, as manuscript memories failed, the two thespians turned to Shakespeare, which was easier to bullshit their way through. The old English, outdated even in its own time, was hard for the modern ear to follow, particularly as out-of-context snippets. If winging it threw the duo off course and into the realm of nonsense, nobody called them on it, and the steady drip of cash did not diminish.

For their most lucrative stretch of The Bard, Craig played Othello, the Moor of Venice. It was casting against type since the two-man show already had someone better qualified to play a Moor. But Craig knew most of his lines and Maziar did not, so they deferred to the text and ran the risk of race swapping. It wasn't an issue. Most of the audience didn't even realize they were doing Shakespeare, but enough of them were impressed to see park panhandlers shooting for a more cultured spectacle than bad beatboxing or off-key folk tunes strung on an out-of-tune pawnshop guitar. By lunchtime, when the sur-rounding office buildings emptied out, and the investment bankers and day-traders went to brown-bag it in some green space, the pizza box saw a lot of traffic. The markets were up that day, and the finan-cial-district drones were feeling generous. A novelty act was all it took to inspire them to dispose of their spare change from food-truck purchases and vending machine return slots.

By mid-afternoon, once the last of the power lunches had fizzled out, Craig and Maziar called an intermission to count their box-office take. There was an extended debate about how far their proceeds would carry them, and if it was worth risking an en-core in order to capitalize on the return-trip rush hour at the end of the day.

Craig's point that they were both missing their passports—real or forged—limited their travel op-tions. Even if they were to risk a flight that would require identification, passage out of the country was a sure way to get themselves flagged. Once it was agreed they needed to keep the next hop of their journey domestic, the farthest destinations possible were narrowed down to Hawaii or Alaska. Alaska won the second round of debate. Hawaii was an island trap if they couldn't stow away on a ship des-tined for more exotic ports once they marooned themselves there. Alaska, on the other hand, offered plenty of unobserved and unguarded border by which to enter Canada via the Yukon. If they were up for an

ambitious wilderness hike and were reasonably confi-
dent they wouldn't get eaten by wolves along the way,
they could both be in a whole other country by the
end of the week. All that remained was for them to
cab it to the airport and buy a couple of tickets on the
cheapest no-frills carrier they could find.

A stop at a dollar store allowed them to invest
part of their take in a bag of coin-roll wraps so they
could better arrange their windfall into spendable
denominations that would be acceptable at points of
purchase. Their cab driver was less than thrilled to be
paid in rolls of dimes and nickels. The rolls of quarters and single-dollar bills were less of a problem at
the ticket kiosk for the ill-named Icar-US Air. The
airline was approaching insolvency, and the vendor
was a pleasant young woman who was glad to still
have a paying job, even as she candidly wondered if
she'd get to keep her sharp blue uniform once her
employers filed for Chapter 11. It was likely the only
severance pay she could look forward to.

With no check-in bags or carry-ons, Craig and
Maziar sailed through security and kept a low profile
in the passenger lounge as they waited for their flight
to be called. They used their final roll of quarters to
buy a couple of magazines to hide behind in their
seats, avoiding eye contact with fellow passengers and
security cameras until it was time to board the plane.

It was only once the Airbus A220 finished taxiing
around the tarmac, straightened out on a runaway,
and kicked the twin engines to full thrust, that Craig

and Maziar began to breathe easy. Pressed into their seats by the steady acceleration, they were soon in the sky and climbing ever higher, banking north towards a remote land where no one could possibly recognize them and, if their good fortune held out, no one would ever find them.

Once the plane levelled out and they reached cruising altitude, Maziar counted the nest egg that remained for them to launch their new lives as un-documented political refugees.

"Better opt for a soda when the drinks cart comes around," he told Craig. "Anything harder will bankrupt us."

"I guess we'll have to thumb a ride into town once we land."

"How cold do you think it will be up there?"

"Colder than we're dressed for," said Craig. "Probably not cold enough for us to die of exposure before we can find a Goodwill good enough to set us up with some thermal underwear."

"We're going to stick out like the biggest pair of half-assed tourists they've ever seen."

"A couple of pairs of boots, two coats, we'll blend in. I haven't shaved in days, so I'm halfway to looking like an authentic mountain man. You…"

Craig took another look at Maziar with a more critical eye.

"You might stick out more," he concluded.

"I've been asked to play just about every darker-skinned ethnicity on record," Maziar said. "Maybe I can get by as an Eskimo."

"I think they're called 'Inuit' now," said Craig. "You better know that if you're going to pass for an Eskimo."

"Any thoughts on how we're going to make a living next door to the North Pole?"

"Maybe I'll try to get work as a fisherman."

"What if the lakes are frozen?"

"Then I'll see if they're hiring ice fishermen."

"You know anything about catching fish?"

"The kind that are in the water or under the ice?"

"Either."

"I guess I'm going to have to learn. Unless the Arctic Circle is a community-theatre hotbed."

Craig had never been more than a stone's throw past the 49th parallel, and Maziar considered Scotland to be the most desolate northern clime he ever cared to see. Alaska and the territories beyond were an intriguing unknown, to be viewed with an equal mix of excitement and trepidation. Only several hours away, they wondered if they would be greeted by the eerie green glow of the northern lights as the plane descended in the dark of the long night.

They barely made it out of the state, let alone the lower forty-eight. Not more than a couple of hundred miles into their flight path, the airliner was intercepted by a pair of F-16 fighter jets that pulled up to both port and starboard. They matched the velocity of the plane and remained several wing spans away, but both jets were unambiguously in violation of FAA minimum-safe-distance regulations. Whatever communication passed between Air Force interceptors and commercial airliner over the radio resulted in a throttling down of the engines. With the reduced air speed came a discernable dip in altitude, and the Airbus began a rapid decent that lay somewhere between routine final approach and emergency landing.

Craig and Maziar were in one of the three-seat rows on the starboard side. Maziar was able to lean over the woman in the seat next to him to get a better look out the window. Craig unbuckled himself and stood in the aisle so he could look out the opposite window of the double-seat row. There was a man in the way, his nose practically pressed to the glass as he stared at the fighter jet to port that remained in their air space.

"What the hell's going on?" Craig asked no one in particular.

The person blocking the view turned and his eyes widened in horror when he spotted Craig hovering over him. He leaned over to peer around him and quickly found Maziar in his company.

"Two targets," whispered the man hoarsely. His face was ashen, his mouth dry.

"Felix?" said Craig, recognizing the passenger in the window seat. "What are you doing here?"

"I knew I should have flown Delta," was all he said in reply.

14

THEY WERE ON THE GROUND fifteen minutes later.

The airport they had been escorted to was not civilian. Far out in the boonies, there were few roads in evidence, and no traffic on any of them. As the airliner made its descent, the twin F-16s peeled off, ignited their afterburners, and vanished from sight behind the tree line that filled the horizon as the last couple hundred feet of altitude bled away.

Even as the airborne chaperones withdrew, they were relieved by their earthbound counterparts. The moment the plane's wheels touched down on the tarmac, multiple cars and trucks appeared along the fringes of the runway and accelerated to keep pace with the landing aircraft as it slowed to a languid taxiing pace. There was no terminal to be directed to, nor any of the typical airport trappings to service a commercial jet. Instead, the plane took a sharp right turn at the end of the runway and rolled into an enormous hangar before cutting its engines and coming to a full stop.

Over the confused and worried murmurs of the other passengers, Craig could hear the rattle of the hangar doors closing and sealing behind them. Most of the natural daylight was shut out, and overhead floods came on, revealing the airliner was the sole occupant of the facility.

There had been no announcement by the pilot, and the flight attendants had vanished from their stations soon after the midair interception. Call buttons had not been responded to prior to landing, and the sole hint of communication with the travellers in the fuselage was the overhead seatbelt icon lighting up. Now that they were landed and stopped, the passengers grew fussy and irritable. Seatbelts were coming off and people were standing, using the toilets, and speculating wildly.

Before they could become too belligerent, a single rolling staircase trundled up to the foremost port door of the plane and one of the cabin crew finally appeared to help unseal it. She ignored the questions asked of her, leaving the lone man who stepped inside once the door was open to respond to all concerns in a booming voice that could be heard all the way in the back.

"Ladies and gentlemen, I am Lieutenant Colonel Corruthers and would kindly ask for your attention please."

The chatter throughout the plane simmered down at the prospect of having the situation explained at last.

"Your flight has been interrupted on a matter of national security," he continued. "We're going to have to ask you all to deplane for a short time while we confirm identifications and make background checks. Please leave your carry-on luggage behind and proceed to the front of the cabin with any papers you have on your person. I assure you, the delay will be a brief one, and we'll be sending you on your way shortly. I thank you for your cooperation, as does Homeland Security."

With no further elaboration, the officer turned and headed back down the stairs, leaving the emerging crew of the plane in charge of corralling their passengers through the door and onto the steps that would allow them to reassemble on the floor of the hangar.

Craig, Maziar, and Felix fought the urge to bolt. There was nowhere to run to on the plane. All the other doors were sealed, and even if they could figure out how to get one open before they were detained, it was a long drop that promised broken ankles and another closed space to escape from. This one full of armed Air Force personnel.

Through an exchange of low whispers and angry accusations, it was finally agreed upon than they should cooperate for the moment and see how things played out. Maziar optimistically suggested that maybe the unscheduled landing had nothing to do with them, and it was merely in response to a tip about a ticking bomb in the baggage compartment that was moments away from blowing them all back into the sky. This time in tiny pieces. Craig and Felix weren't sold, much as they wished they could see the same silver lining.

Passengers were sorted one by one as they stepped off the staircase. Most were filtered to the left, where they were being directed out a side door in the hangar by small squads of soldiers, a dozen at a time. More soldiers waited on the right. Those amounted to only four men, and so far no one had been assigned to them. There was no ambiguity as to who they were there for, however. From the top of the stairs, Craig spotted Warren Wolcott among the armed men, waiting patiently for his wayward crisis actors to be culled from the herd.

Craig almost waved, the reunion was so inevitable. Eye contact from fifty feet away sufficed.

At the bottom of the stairs, Craig didn't even wait for the sorting soldiers to wave him right. He removed himself from the line and headed towards Wolcott of his own accord. Maziar had to be told to take a right-hand turn, which he obeyed. Felix Hinch went left with all the rest and didn't question it. He wasn't a fan of either option, but was certain no good could come of being singled out. Following the civilian masses, Felix didn't dare offer Craig and Maziar a goodbye or even a single glance for fear of admitting an association to the guards all around them.

"Is all this for us?" Craig asked Wolcott, once he'd arrived face-to-face with him.

"Oh dear boy," chortled the senator, "you make it sound like a major operation. Waylaying a single commercial flight is only ever a phone call away."

"Senator," Maziar nodded politely as he joined Craig.

"How did you find us?" asked Craig.

"We were so careful," said Maziar.

"You did well for a couple of amateurs," Wolcott assured them. "But we knew it was only a matter of time before you pinged our radar. Especially if you were foolish enough to stick together. Run enough searches for such a combo and we were bound to turn up something sooner rather than later."

"We should have split up," said Craig. It was so obvious in retrospect, but being on the run all alone had been too horrible to consider.

"Don't beat yourself up, son. That would have only kept you two at large for another few hours at best."

"When did you spot us?" asked Maziar.

"Airport security cameras told us what flight you were on, but we'd been tracking you long before that. I wouldn't have guessed that the first sighting our algorithms identified would be a cameo appearance on a Chaturbate livestream, but it seems there are cameras everywhere these days. Even in our bedrooms. Orwell predicted as much, but I doubt even he anticipated that so many private citizens would invite the cameras into their homes and point them at themselves willingly."

"So what happens to us now?" Craig asked.

"This is where you and your friend part ways at last," said Wolcott.

He turned to Maziar, who was taken politely but firmly by two soldiers, one on each arm.

"We have a connecting flight waiting for you," the senator informed him. "We will reconvene at a later date."

Maziar was the final passenger to be led away, this time through a door to the right. The flight crew, directed left with the other civilians, disappeared out of their own exit. Wolcott nodded to the remaining men under his command and they promptly marched away, leaving Craig and the senator alone in the huge hangar.

"How are you going to explain this unscheduled landing?" Craig asked. "It sounds like a lot of lawsuits in the making."

"No one is suing anyone," the senator confidently asserted. "This landing never happened. There was no plane to set down anywhere, and wherever it ended up, it wasn't here."

"What happened to it?" Craig asked, looking over his shoulder at the parked airliner that was so conspicuously present.

"It crashed of course," he was told. "Twenty minutes ago. No survivors, I'm afraid. A plane that big nose dives into the ground, you can't hope for any miracles."

"The plane is right here," Craig reminded him.

"And here it shall remain," replied Senator Wolcott. "But the crash site is wherever we say it is. We haven't decided yet. Someplace suitably remote. The media will point their cameras at whatever debris field we tell them to. The NTSB report is being written as we speak, with a release date set for this time next year. We'll burn some tires for smoke, throw a few cans of gasoline on for that distinct fuel stink, and add a couple of steaks to get the charred-flesh smell in the air. The results are very convincing."

"Where are the rest of the passengers?" Craig asked, suddenly concerned.

Wolcott consulted his wristwatch.

"Right about now? Being machine gunned at the bottom of a pit, doused in accelerant, and set ablaze. Any remains will be chemically dissolved and poured into the nearest river with an ocean outlet."

"What about the women and children?"

"Especially the women and children. More sympathy for the scope of the tragedy that way. Don't feel bad for them. It was their poor luck getting on the same flight as you. And there are worse things than dying with your loved ones. It's the U.M.'s in these situations that tug at the heart strings."

"The ums?"

"Unaccompanied Minors. I like to take those aside, buy them a candy bar, and reassure them they'll be escorted home shortly. Then I pay someone in security a little extra to shoot them in the back of the head when they least expect it. It's kinder that way."

Wolcott brightened up a moment later.

"Anyway, no U.M.'s on this flight, thank goodness. Just you and your fellow dissident to be dealt with."

"But there were children aboard."

"There are always children," said Wolcott. "Even when there isn't. When we stage a crash, we're always careful to scatter around a few burnt dolls. The media loves shots of burnt dolls. It's not a real body, but you can picture the little girl who clung to it as the plane went down. She was killed instantly, but the doll lives forever in some The-Year-in-Pictures retrospective."

"You'll never fool all the families!" Craig insisted. "They'll demand remains for funerals."

"We have an arrangement with the Chinese," the senator told him. "Body parts for depleted uranium. I think we're getting the raw end of the deal, but clean untraceable body parts are a valuable commodity. Once they're done harvesting organs from their political prisoners, they ship us the leftovers on demand and we parse out the bits and pieces to grieving families in these situations."

"Doesn't anyone check that what you gave them is who you say it is?"

"Nobody asks for a second opinion on post-mortem DNA tests. Especially when all they're getting back to bury are three teeth, a femur, and two toes. It's symbolic, really. Nobody cares so long as there's a nice tombstone to visit on Mother's Day, Father's Day, birthdays, etcetera."

"What have you done with Maziar?"

"Don't worry, he's fine," said the senator. "We still have plans for him."

"And Felix?"

"Felix?"

"Someone else I know," explained Craig. "You cut him loose at The Grove."

"Ah, him!" Wolcott recalled. "Felix Hinch is one of ours."

"That can't be true!" Craig protested. "Nobody is that good an actor."

"He's not acting. He genuinely thinks he washed out of the program. But not only did Felix Hinch make the grade, he's been one of our most successful crisis actors."

"Felix is a crisis actor, too?"

"Oh yes," replied the senator. "A success story second only to your own."

"Impossible!"

"Not all the controlled opposition know they're controlled," Wolcott explained. "It pays to have a certain number of wild conspiracy theories out there, broadcast by their vocal proponents. The right mix of the truth and crazy ramblings and nobody can figure out which is which. Hinch has been a very useful idiot. Best of all, he's been working for free. Other than a few handling expenses here and there, nudging him in the right direction, planting certain incorrect notions in his head, he's been our top cost/benefit asset."

"You'll let him go then," Craig suggested hopefully.

Senator Wolcott shook his head slowly.

"Even useful idiots get used up eventually. Then it's time to make sure they stay dumb forever."

"This is all my fault," Craig said, staring at his hands like there was blood dripping off them. "I got everyone killed just getting on that fucking plane!"

"Console yourself it wasn't a sold-out flight," said Wolcott.

"Oh my God!" Craig moaned.

For a moment, Senator Wolcott thought it was more self-indulgent guilt. An actor acting regret. Then he saw what his thespian had spotted in the hangar with them. It was a little girl. Eight years old at most. She had become separated from the rest of the passengers and had somehow gotten back inside, unnoticed.

"You shouldn't wander away from your parents like that," Wolcott told her. "It's a big airport and you could get lost."

"I'm thirsty," said the girl.

"Oh, it's a drink you're after. Well, then, come along and let's see if we can't find a water cooler to quench that thirst."

Wolcott held out his hand like an uncle or grandfather might and the girl took it. Craig remained frozen to the spot, unable to move, words caught in this throat.

The senator led the child to a vending machine standing against a wall. It was plugged into a socket next to an office that looked out over the hangar floor.

"Ah, just the thing," he said. "Do you like ginger ale, cola, or maybe a root beer?"

"My mommy doesn't like me to have fizzy drinks. She says they make me wet the bed."

"This can be our little secret," Wolcott gently assured her, "and I promise there will be no bedwetting tonight."

He dug into his pocket and found four quarters to feed the machine. A can of Coke clunked into the outlet slot. Wolcott retrieved it, opened it, and handed it to the girl. She was only a couple of sips in when one of the soldiers came marching back from guard duty.

"We're just about done, sir," he reported. "This is the last one."

Wolcott leaned down and told the girl, "You go with the nice sergeant, dear. He'll send you along to be with your mother."

She obeyed her elder and followed the uniformed man out, sipping away at her can of carbonated sugar water.

"So sad, so tragic," said the senator softly as he watched them go.

Wolcott returned to Craig's side and waited while his lead actor struggled to find the words. When he rediscovered his voice at last, there was only one question on his mind.

"Why am I still alive?"

"We can't kill you," Wolcott said, like it was painfully obvious to state out loud. "You know too much."

"Isn't that the best reason to kill someone?"

"Your thinking is so narrow," the senator admonished, "You know too much, so we have to keep you alive to extract all those things you know."

"But I don't know anything you don't already know! I've only ever done what you asked me to do!"

"I understand that, my boy. I do. But these things must be confirmed, recorded, and verified. Only once we've done all that can they be denied, redacted, and disavowed."

"You're going to torture me, aren't you?" Craig practically shouted as the fear crept in.

"We don't do that sort of thing here," Wolcott said. "It never works, and we've done enough morally ambiguous things on American soil for one day. The kind of questions we have for you, we like to ask in places far away, well removed from anyone's jurisdiction."

Craig backed away from the big man and his ill intent, wondering how far he would get if he ran. Before he could even turn around, the running option was taken off the table. Craig found he had backed into a wall of muscle and body armour. Two giant hands clamped down on his shoulders from behind. Another set took hold of one arm, a third the other.

The guidance all those hands offered was surprisingly gentle, even polite in tone. Craig allowed himself to be steered away, knowing the civil touch would strengthen and apply pressure well in excess of what would be needed to ensure compliance. It would hurt like hell, and there would be plenty of opportunity for pain and suffering yet to come.

"Bon voyage," the senator wished him.

15

THE PLANE HE WAS PUT ON had no windows, so Craig couldn't tell where he was going. He spent the flight sedated and strapped to a gurney, and was unable to guess how long he was in the air. The IV drip that was stuck in his arm kept him loopy and he missed the landing entirely, dozing through the touchdown and unloading. As he was the sole piece of cargo, the unloading was quick and efficient. Before everything went completely dark, Craig's dreams were disturbed by the sound of giant propellers roaring back to life as the plane turned back down the barren runway of an airfield so remote, there was no hint of other aircraft, field crew, or service vehicles.

The tone of the distant engines changed as the plane lifted off, and then was cut off entirely as heavy steel doors closed behind him and shut out all sound and light. There was only the squeak of gurney wheels on concrete and the long dim that seemed to stretch out to eternity.

• • •

Craig was conscious and aware again so abruptly he thought he was waking up from a nightmare, only to find he had arrived in a real one, much worse and much brighter. Glaring lights surrounded him and his eyes had a hard time adjusting to his new surroundings. If not for the sharp pain in his arm, he wouldn't have noticed the hypodermic needle being withdrawn from a vein. The injection—whatever was in the chemical cocktail—had worked fast. Any residual fuzziness from the sedative was gone and he was wide awake. Adrenalin, natural or supplemental, surged through his system. They wanted him alert for what came next.

"Where am I?" Craig asked, hoping there was someone present to answer him. Dreading that there was someone in the room to do more than answer him.

"Well, it's not Afghanistan, that's for sure."

It was Brett Wolcott. Craig was glad to see a familiar face, even if it wasn't a friendly one.

"That wouldn't have been my first guess," said Craig.

"It was my first choice," said Brett. "One step closer to picking up where I left off before I got assigned this shit show. But no. The black sites we have there weren't good enough for daddy's favourite protégé. You get the velvet-glove treatment. Only the best."

Craig realized they weren't alone in the room together. He sensed another presence. There was the smell of tobacco burning and Brett wasn't smoking. As his eyes adjusted to the light, he saw someone sitting in the corner.

"Who's there?" Craig asked.

"The best," answered Brett.

Hunched on a stool, nursing a cigarette with no filter and two inches of dangling ash, was a shrivelled Asian man who looked old enough to have retired twice over. Retired from what occupation exactly was the unknown that hung in the air as thick as the smoke in the poorly ventilated room.

"The best at what?"

"The sort of people who are in a position of authority to order people like you and me to black sites like this call it 'enhanced interrogation,'" said Brett. "That's a bullshit term for the squeamish. Whether it's waterboarding or electric shocks, stress positions or sleep deprivation, it's all just torture. Pure and simple."

"Your father told me himself!" protested Craig. "He said torture doesn't work!"

"Of course torture works," replied Brett. "Why do you think we keep telling everybody that torture doesn't work? It's so *we* don't get tortured."

"But don't people just make stuff up to get it to stop?"

"Sure," Brett said, "if they run out of useful information. But before that happens, they'll tell you *everything* else."

"What if I just volunteer information?" Craig suggested. "I'm an open book. Ask me anything. I have nothing to hide. Really!"

"How will we know you're telling the truth? You're an actor."

"Not a very good one, I swear!"

"Don't worry," Brett assured him. "Five minutes from now, you won't be in any condition to put on a show. Then we'll know you're being honest with us."

"Is waterboarding as bad as they say it is?" asked Craig, picturing his gurney tilting back at a sharp angle so the towel and bucket of water could do their worst.

"They do it to us as part of Special Forces training so we know how we would hold up," said Brett. "It sucks."

"It's like drowning, isn't it?"

"It *is* drowning," Brett specified. "It's drowning without the dying at the end of it part. That way they can do it to you over and over again."

"I don't want to be waterboarded!" Craig cried, tears moistening his face before his torturer could splash a single drop on him.

"You're not getting waterboarded," Brett promised him. "No stress positions, no sleep deprivation.

Nhung doesn't do any of that shit. He's old school. Hardcore."

At the mention of his name, the ancient Asian rose from his stool and took a moment to balance himself on his arthritic feet. A coughing fit threw off that hard-won balance and it took him twice as long to regain his footing. Once he was mobile, he tottered over to a counter with a tray that was covered in a single sterile sheet of white linen. He pulled it away, like a magician revealing a grand illusion to a paying audience. Craig was the only audience member, but he felt like he was about to be made to pay. And a much higher price than he cared to.

The tray was filled with a wide array of delicate tools in stainless steel. Most of them were either razor sharp or pointed. Somehow, the small number of blunt ones looked even more terrifying.

"Nhung has been at this since Saigon, haven't you Nhung?"

The old man flashed a big toothy grin. It looked kindly.

"He's very good at his job," Brett said.

"So I won't feel a thing, huh?" Craig grimly asked.

"Oh, you'll feel everything. That's what makes him so good."

Nhung took his time considering his opening move before finally selecting something that looked like a curved scalpel that had been made to order by a master craftsman. It was a thing of beauty, designed to do very ugly things.

"I'll leave you two alone to become better acquainted," said Brett, as he removed himself from the interrogation.

Craig wondered if he didn't have the stomach to stay, but realized it was more a matter of him lacking the soul to care.

"What are you going to do?" Craig asked Nhung, his mind racing from one gruesome possibility to the next. "No, let me guess. You're going to break my kneecaps! Or cut off my balls!"

Craig was trying not scream. His eyes were already watering freely as a defense mechanism, like they suspected they might be the first extremity to go under the knife.

"No, no, my friend," said Nhung, patting him on the leg reassuringly. "Nothing so dramatic. You don't understand the art of the thing. The mastery it takes to become a great torturer."

"Maybe just tell me instead of showing me?"

Nhung smiled again, and patiently explained in a relaxed, soothing voice.

"Take away a man's ability to ever walk again, ever fuck again, and he will despair," Nhung said sagely. "Many will consider life no longer worth living, and anything you do after that is ineffective. You must never open with castration—must never begin a session by shattering legs or degloving hands or peeling off faces. It is too much, too soon. A subject must always dread what you will do to him next. If you take something too vital away from him, he loses all hope. With no hope, there can be no dread. And without dread, torture is only pain for pain's sake."

Craig recognized an artist talking about his craft. He'd heard that sort of meditation before in acting classes, or coming out of his own mouth when trying to explain his vocation to a neophyte.

"Once you have all you came for," continued Nhung, "know all there is to know, you may indulge yourself in such finishing touches. For personal satisfaction, for punishment, as you wish. By then, the job should be done. The rest is recreation."

Craig also recognized a sadist talking about his fetish. He'd heard some of that in the business as well. Usually from producers.

"Shall we begin now?" Nhung asked, as though he were genuinely seeking permission.

"No need to rush things," said Craig.

"No," Nhung agreed. "No, not at all."

He contemplated the instrument in his hand, holding it up to his face, the blade perilously close to the tip of his nose, and re-evaluated his choice. Thinking better of it, he returned to his tray, set the blade back in its original position, and considered a pair of pliers instead.

Craig's muscles instinctively bucked as his brain leapt to the immediate future and envisioned the coming agony. It was like the scalpel was already digging in, the pliers already pinching, so clear was this vision. The anticipation of pain was almost as bad as the pain itself, and served as an integral part of the torture.

As his right arm violently twitched at the thought of his palm being slashed, or his fingernails been peeled off, Craig found his range of movement to be broader than he expected. He looked down and saw that one of the straps binding him to the gurney wasn't buckled correctly. The prong had come out of the punch hole. With a single firm pull, Craig was able to free his hand. His other wrist was easy to un-shackle once he had full control of his right arm. A single sit-up put the bindings around his ankles within reach, and they came loose as easily as any standard belt.

By the time Nhung turned around again with his second-guessed tool of torment, Craig was sitting on the edge of the gurney, unbound. Free and not yet certain what to do with that freedom.

"Oh, this won't do," said Nhung of the break in protocol. "You need to be secured for this to work at all. If you move about too much, I might seriously injure you."

His concern was almost touching, and Craig felt genuinely bad when he lashed out with his foot, up-percutting Nhung in the jaw and sending him reeling.

Hopping off the gurney, Craig tried the door first, but it wouldn't budge. Cornered, he readied himself to fight a man who looked to be nearly three times his age. It wasn't a proud moment, but he felt self-defence was perfectly warranted in this situation.

What he saw when he turned to face his opponent was a feeble senior citizen, gasping for breath on the floor, trying to sit up and failing repeatedly.

Craig had his fists raised, like a pseudo prize fighter who had never advanced beyond shadow boxing. He dropped his defensive posture when he saw Nhung wasn't getting to his feet any time soon, and was in no state to deliver so much as a paper cut upon the last victim of his prolific career in cruelty. Craig felt bad for the old man. Even after decades of unspeakable sin, he had arrived at the final stage of his life a helpless, weak ghost of what he had once been. It inspired enough pity for Craig to at least help him up and let him preserve some small dignity.

"Okay," said Craig, bending down and taking Nhung by the arm, "let's get you on the gurney. Is there a doctor around here somewhere?"

Nhung coughed and wheezed as he nodded, before finally confirming, "I am a doctor."

"Yeah," Craig acknowledged, "I was thinking more of the kind that patches people up rather than takes them apart."

"I will be all right," Nhung assured him. "Let me have a cigarette to catch my breath."

"Seriously? Looks like those things are killing you."

"Life kills all. Smoking makes the time we spend waiting for death more tolerable."

Craig didn't argue the point. He reached into the old man's cardigan to retrieve his pack of cigarettes for him. Nhung still had a firm hold on his pair of pliers and used that moment to strike at Craig like a snake. With a single fluid motion of unerring accuracy, he found Craig's left nipple, hidden under his shirt, and clamped down on it hard. Craig screamed.

"Very sensitive area," Nhung hissed at him, informatively. "Many nerve endings."

Craig rose to his feet so forcefully, he pulled Nhung up with him by the nipple-and-pliers coupling. The agony made his knees lock and his fists clench hard enough, he thought he would drive his own fingernails through the backs of his hands. He remained fixed in this position until Nhung started twisting the pliers, and that was enough to force Craig's instinct of self-preservation to kick in. He shoved Nhung off him and the pliers came free, almost taking the nipple with them. Craig looked down and felt like he was lactating blood. The pain was pinpoint sharp and red dots stained through his shirt. Rubbing the sore spot did nothing to lessen the sting, but served to spread it around so it became a more generalized ache across his entire chest.

Nhung hit a wall hard, but it stopped his fall and kept him on his feet. He advanced again, his pliers looking for a new sensitive nerve cluster to latch on to. Craig didn't wait to find out where the next target on his body might be.

The old man's tools were within arm's reach. None had any heft to them; all were small and made for precision. Rather than think too hard about which one would be best suited for melee combat, Craig chose all of them at once, gripping the corners of the tray and flinging the entire contents at Nhung.

The implements tumbled through the air end over end. Most of those ends were sharp, and at least half of them struck Craig's tormentor tip first, allowing them to penetrate and stick. Nhung froze in place, a pincushion showcase of the finest steel his trade had to offer. If he felt any pain, he betrayed none of it. The only thing his wide, staring eyes conveyed was shock, and perhaps a sudden onset of a pre-existing medical condition that took the bodily trauma as a cue to manifest itself all at once.

Nhung dropped his pliers. They were in mid-bounce off the floor when his body followed, collapsing as though the many points he'd been struck by had severed all his tendons at the same time.

Craig dared not approach the old man crumpled on the floor for fear it was a ruse. He left that task to Brett Wolcott, who burst through the door to see what the commotion was. Brett ignored Craig and rushed to Nhung's side, feeling for a pulse and checking the size of his fixed pupils. There were eight pins stuck in him, four blades, and three needles—plus forceps, an extended box cutter, a dental pick, and a small pair of scissors. None of them looked very deep. It was hard to imagine the wounds were mortal.

"Goddammit, you killed Nhung," Brett concluded.

"It was him or me!" said Craig.

"You asshole, he needed this job. He had a whole family to feed."

"What? His great-grandchildren? He must be ninety years old!"

"He was a widower. Four times over," said Brett. "His wives kept dying and he kept remarrying. Younger each time. His current wife just had twins."

"This guy was still pumping out kids at his age?"

"Not anymore, thanks to you."

Brett left Nhung's body on the floor to be processed and returned to his family by someone else. He had more pressing issues to deal with.

"Why didn't you just leave?" he asked Craig.

"The door was locked."

Brett shut the door, latched it, unlatched it, and opened it again with no further explanation. The mechanics of the latch were simple enough, but in his initial panic of flight, Craig had failed to extrapolate the simple series of manoeuvres that would have paved an easy path for him. Realizing the door was never locked helped Craig leap to an obvious conclusion.

"You were the one who loosened the straps," he said. "You let me escape."

"No, I let you go," Brett specified.

"So I could escape."

"So you could get shot trying to escape."

"You want me dead?"

"Everyone wants you dead."

"But you came when you heard me screaming," Craig said.

"I expected to hear you screaming," said Brett. "You were being tortured. It was all the banging and crashing I was checking on."

"Why let me escape just so I could get shot?"

"Call it a difference of opinion about how your case should be handled," said Brett. "Tortured and killed or just killed. Maybe I'm getting soft, but I'd rather go the kinder, gentler route. You earned it. For a douchebag actor, you've been a good sport."

"So what now?" Craig asked.

Brett deliberated on how to handle the situation. It didn't take long.

"We can still consider this an escape situation. What you did to Nhung will help sell the story. Just hang on a minute while I grab a gun."

Craig did not hang on. Remembering he was still gripping the steel tray by one end, he used it, swinging it as hard as he could into Brett's face.

There was no need to fuss with the door this time. It hung open, leading Craig into a dimly lit service tunnel. Regularly spaced lights along the ceiling suggested it ran straight for a mile or more in either direction. With no indication which was the better route, Craig ran left and hoped for the best. After several minutes of listening to his heavy footfalls echo through the tight passage, he guessed he'd traversed the length of two or more football fields and was beginning to suspect he'd chosen wrong. In all that space, there had been no branches, no doors, no hatches. Only the same drab corridor with a light fixture overhead every twenty feet.

It was the absence of one light that broke the pattern. Craig thought the bulb must have burned out, but when he paused in that dark stretch and looked up, he saw no fixture at all. Instead there was a hole—and at the bottom lip of that hole, a rung. Craig leapt up and grabbed hold. The moment he hung his weight on it, an extended ladder rattled down and struck the floor with a sharp thud that was deafeningly amplified by the tunnel. Once it was in place, the climb straight up was made easier, so Craig attempted it, even though there was nothing to see up the shaft but pitch black.

Each time he looked down, the spot of faint illumination from the tunnel he'd left behind was disturbingly smaller. A single misstep would result in a fall that promised a twisted ankle, then broken legs, and finally a snapped neck. And still there were more rungs to scale. Craig judged he was at least a hundred feet up when the shaft abruptly ended. He cracked his skull on the steel cap at the top, nearly causing him to lose his grip.

Once he'd secured himself to the rungs again, Craig felt around in the dark and found the edge of what he'd hit his head on. It was a wheel. He tried turning it, and after a few tugs of resistance, it spun freely. Following several complete revolutions, something clicked, and Craig was able to push up the hatch that barred his way. It hinged back as it opened, and the flood of light and heat that came steaming in felt like it would seer his flesh off.

Craig climbed into the onslaught regardless, and came spilling out the top of the funnel and onto the dry, cracked soil of the surface. The hatch slowly swung back down on its hydraulic hinges and resealed itself. By the time his vision adjusted to the new light levels, Craig found himself lying in a jaundiced landscape that looked even less inviting that the cold corridors of poured concrete and utilitarian lighting he had left behind. He wanted to crawl out of the sweltering heat and back into the death trap he had just escaped, but found he was locked out.

There was nothing else to do but run. So he ran. He didn't know where he was, or where he was running to, but there was no going home again. Home was in the United States of America, and that was back on planet Earth. This place was not Earth.

16

THE FARTHER CRAIG RAN through the harsh wilderness of yellow stone and orange soil, the more he became convinced the Wolcotts had shuttled him straight off the planet to some alien world. Strange prickly mushroom-shaped trees dotted the landscape, alongside flowering tendrils jutting out of smooth squat trunks that resembled organs—some internal, others sexual. There were lizards in evidence, basking on rocks or climbing tree branches, that came in colours Craig had never seen on a reptile. Some of them looked like eels that had only recently evolved enough to come crawling out of the ocean. They seemed reluctant to bother growing a functional set of legs. At least not until they decided to commit to the move.

The sun was so hot, Craig paused a moment, sheltering his eyes so he could look up and confirm there was only one of them. He counted twice more, just to be sure.

After a long scramble through the unforgiving desert, Craig considered finding some shade to rest in for a few moments. The only shadow cast on the ground in his immediate vicinity was his own. When he stared down at it, stretched across the dry dirt, it looked for a moment like the spot where the shape of his head fell was rippling. A distant boom echoed between the ridges a moment later, and Craig hoped it was a peel of thunder promising rain in the near future despite the cloudless sky. When he took another step forward, he saw the place where the ripple had occurred in the full light. He'd originally thought it was an effect of the heat, like a shimmer on the horizon of a hot day, only much closer. But once his shadow had moved, he saw a small hole, surrounded by a rim of disturbed sand.

Craig bent down to inspect the hole he was sure hadn't been there when he'd first stopped to get his bearings. Initially he thought it might be the work of a burrowing insect, but there was no movement to suggest anything digging under the surface. Cautiously, he stuck a finger in the hole and felt something solid and hot—hotter even than the surrounding soil that had been baking under the sun. Pushing some of the crumbling flakes aside, he broadened the hole and stuck his thumb in as well so he could get a grip on the object and pull it free.

Sunlight glinted off the copper finish of the metallic nub as Craig examined the thing. He tossed it up and down in his palm as it cooled and became easier to handle. The cylinder was about the size of a fingertip, with one end that was badly deformed and blunted. By the time he realized he was looking at a spent bullet, there was another impact between his feet. Craig was running again before the report of the distant shot arrived at the speed of sound a couple of seconds later.

Wherever the shooter was hiding, he was perched somewhere on the high ground of the rocky ridges. Given the delay between the impact and the sonic boom of the bullet leaving the rifle barrel, he was far off. But that wasn't keeping him from landing long-range shots that were close enough to put him on the podium of a marksman competition.

Craig tried to cut through a nearby ravine, only to have a shot ricochet off a rock no more than two feet in front of him. Instinctively, he turned around and dashed in the opposite direction, finding himself exposed in open land with no cover. Each time a new shot landed, Craig ran away from the point of impact, zigzagging his way through the alien domain. He had no idea where he was going, but the sniper seemed to anticipate his every move.

Regardless of how fast or how far he ran, Craig was never able to get out of range of the gunman. In only a few minutes, he'd managed to exhaust himself, and at last he had no choice but to drop, gasping, into the first stretch of shade he could find. Sure he was still exposed, still in the crosshairs of a distant rifle scope, Craig backed himself into a jagged rock face under a high cliff and waited for the end. Another few moments of terrified anticipation and then his brains would be blown out the back of his head, solving all his problems once and for all.

The shot didn't come, but the sniper was still out there, watching. A glint of light atop a distant hilltop caught Craig's attention, and he knew it must be the sun reflecting off the lens of the scope. If only he had a weapon of his own, he could return fire. But he knew the chance of him hitting anything at such an extreme range was nil.

The lens flare glinted at him a few more times and then ceased. The sniper rose from his vantage point, collected his equipment, and then started to walk down the lip of the ridge. At this distance, he was little more than a tiny silhouette, barely recognizable as human. But once the man was off the high ground, he slowly grew more distinct, getting closer by the second. Craig knew then that the sniper was coming to confirm his kill, even though he wasn't quite dead yet. Had he any energy left at all, Craig would have sought out a hefty rock he could wield, and tried to find a spot where he could hide in ambush. But there was no point. The shooter had eyes on him, was beelining towards him at a steady march, and Craig had been reduced to gasping for his next lungful of hot air in the wasteland.

A hundred feet out, Craig could tell the approaching gunman was wearing a desert camo uniform and ghillie hat. Fifty feet out, he could see the face under the hat. By the time he was within twenty feet of him, Craig could identify that face. That's when he knew Brett Wolcott's rifle shots hadn't been missing him. They'd been corralling him.

"Here," said Brett, handing him a water canteen. "Sip it slowly or you'll choke."

Craig accepted the canteen and did as he told. However he meant to kill him, apparently Brett Wolcott didn't want him to choke to death.

"Not too much," said Brett, taking the canteen back. "It won't do you much good if you puke it back up."

Whether or not his fate was sealed seemed a moot point. If he was going to die here, Craig only wanted to know where here was. So he asked.

"Where the hell am I?"

Brett stood over him in his camouflage hunting gear and adjusted the rifle slung over his shoulder.

"Yemen," he said.

"This is Yemen?" Craig asked, looking around, trying to reconcile this new piece of information. He still wasn't convinced it was planet Earth.

"It's an island far off the coast of Yemen," specified Brett. "So far off the coast, it's technically in Africa. Soco-something or other."

"We have a secret base in Yemen?"

"We have secret bases all over the place. I guess we wanted one in Yemen, too. Just not in any of the parts we're bombing."

"Why does everything look so weird?"

"If you're going to disappear people, you want to pick someplace remote. This place is so remote, it's evolved its own ecosystem. There are all sorts of species of plants and animals here that don't exist anywhere else."

"Sounds like a choice vacation destination," said Craig. "Where are all the tourists?"

"Nobody goes on holiday in Yemen. We've seen to that."

"I'm tired of running," Craig wheezed.

"Good, because we're there."

"There where?"

Brett pulled his rifle off his shoulder and pointed the barrel at a simple plain door set in the side of the rock face directly behind Craig.

"Your final destination," he said.

17

BRETT HELD THE DOOR OPEN FOR CRAIG. Like the others, it was unlocked. There was no one around to infiltrate, no one to trespass.

Craig pulled himself to his feet and looked inside.

"Is this another black site?" asked Craig.

"No, it's part of the one you just left. We have an ant farm of tunnels running under the surface. I hope you enjoyed some sun and fresh air because you're headed back down. Deep down."

Craig stared into the void that lay through the door. Even with his vision accustomed to the shade cast by the overhanging cliff, there were no details to be seen inside.

"I'm never coming back, am I?"

"Here lies Craig Linton," Brett announced, "a nobody actor you won't remember from that TV commercial you hated, or that play you never saw. A name that never got famous, with a face that won't ring any bells."

"That's a hell of an epitaph."

"There are worse," said Brett. "Better to be instantly forgotten than hated forever."

Craig stepped through the door, ready to forget and be forgotten. Brett stayed outside and released the door, which swung shut on its own, plunging Craig into total darkness. Alone again, he stood for what seemed like a long time, breathing heavily. He could hear every inhale and exhale in the silence. Each sound reverberated off the walls, but it was impossible to determine how big the room was from the ambient sound alone.

Gears far away began to grind as something approached from below. A slight glow flickered around the seams of a panel in the floor until it lifted straight up to allow an elevator to rise to the surface level. Headlights on a four-wheel vehicle inside the lift blinded Craig until the pilot switched off the high beams, reducing the brightness enough to permit normal sight.

The big man in the driver's seat tapped the horn on the steering wheel a couple of times so a merry "beep-beep" punctuated his arrival. He leaned back and waited for Craig to speak first.

"Nice wheels," he commented.

"I like them, too," said Senator Wolcott.

"Military vehicle?"

"It is now."

"It looks like a golf cart."

"It *is* a golf cart. I got our armed forces to requisition one and ship it in, just for me."

Craig noted the vanity plate screwed to the front bumper.

SEN8R

"I could never get the hang of those personnel transport things the Pentagon orders in bulk."

"Where are we going?" Craig asked, climbing into the passenger seat.

"Down."

"So I'm told."

"Then about a quarter mile south. We could walk it, but somebody didn't budget for an interior decorator, so there's nothing to see but solid rock and concrete. Very boring. The quicker we can get through it, the better."

"Let's get this over with," agreed Craig.

"That's the spirit!" said the senator, and used the grip of a putter to stab at the down button on the elevator's simple control panel.

The elevator clattered down the shaft at a slow steady pace, like a tedious amusement park ride everyone skipped on their way to the Tilt-a-Whirl. There was nothing to do but wait it out.

"This has been a most extraordinary of extraordinary renditions," said Senator Wolcott, "but it's time to stop screwing around and get to work."

"There's a job left to do?" Craig asked.

"Oh yes, we'll be keeping you quite busy this afternoon."

Craig couldn't reconcile what he'd just been through with whatever service they were planning on pressing him into this time.

"What was all the torture about?"

"Did anyone lay a hand on you?"

"Not really," Craig admitted. His nipple ached, but he had suffered worse in routine medical examinations and trips to the dentist.

"Of course not!" said the senator. "We need you fit and unharmed for the shoot. But stressed, sweaty, rattled…that works well for our purposes. Given recent events, we weren't sure you would be willing or able to give us the performance we need, but you should be in the correct frame of mind now. Consider it Method Acting without all the self-indulgent nonsense."

Once the elevator arrived at the only stop, at the bottom of the shaft, Wolcott's golf cart made good time, zipping them down the featureless corridor until they came to a large sealed chamber at the end of the line. As soon as they were through the double doors and the senator parked their ride, Craig knew what they wanted from him.

The setting was familiar. By now, he knew that artificial dune well, backed by a green screen and lit like it was sunny exterior. There was a camera and a crew ready to go. The only difference from the previous set-up was that this crew was all wearing marine uniforms and sidearms.

"Rather more expensive than our set up in Arizona," said the senator, "but here you won't find a Greyhound to spirit you away if you get stage fright again."

A couple of the marines approached the cart to escort Craig to the costume department.

"I'll see you on set," he was told, and the big man went to issue the soldiers under his command their final orders.

An orange jumpsuit was waiting backstage, along with hair and makeup professionals recruited from the ranks. The room was filled with at least a hundred reference photos of Craig pulled from video frames of the previous shoots. They allowed his hair and beard stubble to be coifed into a precise match with the footage released to the public thus far. Once continuity was satisfied with the results, Craig was brought out to the stage floor where the cadre of black-robed terrorists had been reassembled—called back to duty one last time.

While Craig was being outfitted, Senator Wolcott had undergone his own costume change. He had on his clear-plastic raincoat and rubber boots, like he was expecting a soggy day again. This time he would not be denied.

"Take three," Wolcott announced as he sat himself down in a director's chair. "Let's make this the golden one, shall we?"

Craig knew his mark, even though it was half a world away from its counterpart used in previous takes. No one had given him any directions or attempted to instruct him in any way, but he knew what was expected of him and didn't resist. He didn't feel present in the moment as he knelt in the sand, and wondered if the out-of-body experience he was having would help sell the performance even better than in prior attempts.

Someone approached him from behind, and he felt a warm hand on his shoulder and a cold blade on his neck. Craig didn't bother to turn around to confirm who it was. He knew who it had to be.

"Hey, Maziar."

"Hi," replied his co-star, his voice thin and nervous.

"You know, it just occurred to me," said Craig. "This act we've been doing has lasted more shows than any play I've ever been in."

Maziar wasn't interested in Craig's observations about the fickle nature of the craft they so loved.

"I gotta do it, man," he said, the sharp knife quivering in his hand. "I'm sorry. They threatened my family. My kids. They said they would get my SAG card revoked."

"I know," Craig assured him. "Don't sweat it. It was always going to wind up here. They saw to that. I'm done trying to fight it."

The absolution wasn't comforting, but it allowed Maziar to shore himself up for what was to come next. His knife hand stopped shaking, and he took a grip on Craig's hair so firm, it made him forget about his pinched nipple. Craig ignored the pain. In a few more moments, his discomfort would briefly intensify, and then it would be gone forever.

"Everyone in position?" Senator Wolcott asked. "That's splendid. Camera and sound rolling? Right then, everyone get ready. And…action!"

Maziar's blade broke the skin and Craig closed his eyes, waiting for the knife to slice through arteries and trachea until there was nothing holding his head on but spine and sinew. He hoped the blood would rush out of his head fast enough to induce unconsciousness in the first few moments. Craig didn't fancy living long enough to hear Wolcott call "cut," and he certainly wasn't interested in attending the after party.

Before Maziar could dig any deeper than a nick, the shoot was interrupted by a deafening cacophony of shouts and bangs. For a moment, Craig's numb mind thought of Chinese New Year, with strings of firecrackers going off all around and merry cries of delight. These cries weren't delightful, however. They sounded like unintelligible orders barked at men who were not expected to understand or obey.

Craig only dared look once the noise died down. The masked terrorists were all dead and lying in heaps around him. They had been replaced by another squad of masked men. These ones wore balaclavas, not scarves, and were armed with rifles, not knives.

"Cut!" was the next barked order, and the first one Craig understood. Only then did he realize he had lived long enough to hear Senator Wolcott call an end to the scene after all.

None of the dead men got up. They maintained their position and continued soaking the sand dune red with their blood. Craig admired their dedication to their craft until he was forced to accept that no one was acting.

It was the glistening blob resting on the shoulder of his prison jumper that dragged him back to reality. It held Craig's attention as the military unit confirmed their kills, often with additional rounds to the heart and head. It wasn't until after the last coup de grâce was delivered that he successfully identified the clinging bit of fleshy pulp to be a piece of Maziar's brain. Slowly he lifted his trembling fingers to the grey matter and flicked it off and out of sight.

The team leader approached Craig, waving the smoking muzzle of his weapon inches from his face. He passed a hand in front of his eyes several times until the actor became unfrozen and reacted.

Craig looked up at the man, who pulled down his mask and revealed himself.

"Is that a wrap?" Brett Wolcott asked. He was staring directly at Craig, but the question wasn't for him.

"That's a wrap," confirmed Senator Wolcott, as he watched the playback on a video monitor.

Brett slowly raised his rifle to the lone survivor's forehead. Craig shut his eyes again, waiting for his reward for compliance. It would be more merciful than a slit throat, and he was grateful for it.

He felt the steel of the barrel, still hot from discharging half the contents of the rifle's magazine, parting his hair. Craig felt something sharp scraping across his scalp, until it became dislodged from his locks as Brett nudged it away with the end of his weapon. The object fell and landed in the sand. Craig looked at the thing and saw the parts that weren't smeared in blood looked white. He guessed it was a fragment of skull.

"Showers are through that door," Brett instructed him.

Craig rose slowly on wobbly knees. The sifting dune under his feet didn't help keep him steady. He shuffled forward until he was clear of the set and on solid floor that wasn't gritty with sand or slick with blood. Behind him, bodies were already being removed and fitted for bags. No one concerned themselves with Craig, who was alive and well and in no immediate need of disposal.

He stripped out of his stained jumper and threw it into an empty hamper, along with his t-shirt and boxers. The pressure in the showers was excellent, the hot water instant. Craig adjusted the valves so he had a flow and temperature to his liking and then stood motionless under the cascade until he could feel his fingers turn pruney. There was soap, but he made no attempt to wash, only soak. At last he turned the water off and stood dripping wet in front of the wall of mirrors over the sinks, staring at himself intently for a long time, unable to convince himself everything was intact.

He was all right, he concluded. Unblemished, untouched, expect for the one tiny cut Maziar had managed to inflict on him in the moment before the mass execution. The only substantial injury he sustained was to the back of his head when he collapsed to the floor a moment later in a dead faint. Even then, it was only a minor concussion.

18

CRAIG WOKE UP IN A HOSPITAL. At least it looked like a hospital. After being attended to by a doctor, checked on by three different nurses, and having his vitals closely monitored for twelve hours straight, Craig came to realize he was on another set. It was an authentic set, with real state-of-the-art medical equipment, but the hospital stretched no farther than the single patient room. There was a window, with a backdrop that suggested the room was at least ten floors up, but the illusion was spoiled when the last of the three nurses took a wrong turn and walked right past the window's exterior, like she was effortlessly levitating across the sky.

Craig let it slide. It may have been fake, but the care was real, and the nurses had been kind. When the lights dimmed, simulating sunset, Craig let himself sleep, content that no one was trying to kill him for the moment.

The next day he had a visitor. Senator Wolcott brought flowers.

"Feeling better?" he asked.

"Surprised to be feeling anything at all," said Craig. "Where am I? No one tells me anything."

"We've relocated you to another facility. Not such an extraordinary rendition this time. More of a puddle jump."

"Another black site?"

"More of a white site. Like it?"

"No one's tried to torture me or shoot me or cut off my head so far."

"Good lad!" said the senator. "You keep counting those blessings."

"It's not over, is it?"

"Is it ever?"

"No," said Craig.

It wasn't over. Would never be over. But whatever it was, Craig no longer feared it.

19

SENATOR WOLCOTT RETURNED to collect him the next day. He brought a wheelchair, even though Craig felt steady enough to walk. The senator wouldn't hear of it, insisting on pushing the star crisis actor himself. There was a personal appearance to be made, and it was important they weren't late.

A nurse had been by first thing in the morning to give him a sponge bath and a shave. The cut on his neck didn't even warrant a Band-Aid, but she'd applied a fresh coat of a clear antiseptic with a cotton swab. He napped after finishing a tray of toast and breakfast cereal, and woke up to find a three-piece suit draped across the end of his bed. Craig was eager to get out of his revealing hospital gown, and found the clothes that had been left for him fit better than any suit he'd ever worn. Even the one he'd had tailored for a wedding. By the time Wolcott came for him, he felt like a new man, which was appropriate because the senator was there to inform him he was now officially someone else.

Joseph William Kinney was the person he had become. It took a moment for Craig to recall the name, it felt so long since he'd first heard it. He was the fictional diplomat the actor had been pressed to play repeatedly over the past weeks. Craig had only ever heard the name spoken aloud in the context of the news-network interview he'd recorded after the initial beheading. The man only existed in official documents forged on his behalf. Now that he had been saved through the miraculous intervention of a brave navy SEAL team, Joe Kinney had been summoned into a physical body that retired actor Craig Linton would inhabit.

"You're a hero, my boy," Craig was informed.

"I thought I was supposed to be a victim."

"A last-minute rewrite flipped that," said the senator as he rolled Craig across a barren warehouse, from one set to the next. There had been no hospital corridor outside his fake hospital room. "Now you're a hero for having survived your terrible ordeal. You'll be rewarded accordingly."

"Keeping my head is reward enough," Craig assured him.

"Nonsense! It turns out our beheading blooper reel was a stroke of good timing. Now that your story has a happy ending, we're in a position to take full advantage."

Wheeled behind a wall of pressboards and two-by-fours, Craig found himself in a room that was instantly recognizable for what it was supposed to be, rather than what it actually was. For a film set, it was a meticulous recreation that wouldn't have looked out of place in the Smithsonian Institute. Aside from all the furnishings, décor, and wall hangings that looked absolutely authentic, Craig was most surprised to see that the famous office was, in fact, oval shaped.

"Is that who I think it is?" Craig asked of the stately figure standing behind the Resolute Desk.

"It doesn't matter who you think it is, so long as the public is convinced."

"What's he doing here?"

"Politicians like photo ops. Today, you're the hottest photo op in the world."

"Why me? What's happening?"

"You're getting an award," Wolcott told him.

"Not an Oscar by any chance?"

"You're getting the Presidential Medal of Freedom."

"So not an Oscar."

"It's the highest civilian award in the land."

"Then I guess I'm honoured."

"Don't get a big head," Craig was cautioned. "They hand these out like Crackerjack prizes."

The newly minted Joseph William Kinney spent the next twenty minutes getting his photo taken with a sitting president as he was honoured for his patriotic resolve that saw him through such difficult circumstances. They shook hands and made small talk at various points in the office, next to notable busts and treasures from White House history, and in front of the window that looked out at the Rose Garden that wasn't there. Senator Wolcott was asked to step in for a few shots and didn't decline the invitation to pose with his most successful creation.

It was important that the men in the pictures should look relaxed and jovial throughout a series of post-honorific photos that were designed to look spontaneous, if not outright candid. To that end, a professional was brought in to perform for them off-camera so that some genuine smiles and laughter could be captured for newspapers and the inevitable presidential library archives. The funnyman on call looked familiar, but Craig couldn't immediately place him.

"Victor Hurley," Senator Wolcott reminded him. "He's that dwarf comedian who makes jokes about little people and big cocks. He's appearing at a birthday party for a Saudi prince in two days, so we were able to waylay him on short notice to lighten the mood."

The tactic worked. Performed laughter could never match the real thing, and after all he'd been through, Craig needed a good chuckle. Hurley's act did not disappoint, and after the photo shoot was done, Craig made an effort to talk with him, one performer to another, even if he wasn't permitted to reveal his true role in the charade. As far as Victor

Hurley was concerned, this was a well-paid gig that was completely legit, even if the location was a lie.

"I hear you're shooting a movie," said Craig, recalling the last bit of entertainment news he'd heard about the rising star.

"Yeah," said Victor. "Not so sure about making the jump from stand-up to acting, but my agent thinks it's a good idea."

"I'm sure you'll be great."

"I guess you'll be doing your fair share of acting, too."

"What do you mean?" asked Craig, concerned he'd been exposed.

"Aren't they making you an ambassador?"

It was the first Craig had heard about it. Apparently the plans for his future weren't a state secret, even if he was still in the dark. He rolled with it.

"Well, nothing's official yet, but fingers crossed."

"It's a lot of politicking," said Victor. "Meeting dignitaries, making small talk, representing interests. You'll have to put on quite a show."

"I guess you're right," said Craig. "It's all acting."

"And all acting is bullshit."

Victor Hurley raised his bottled water in a toast.

"So from one bullshitter to another, break a leg."

Half of the shoot had been done with Craig in the wheelchair, the other half with him standing using a cane. He didn't need them, and Wolcott insisted on neither once they were done and leaving the set together.

"For a moment there, it was like I was in the real Oval Office," said Craig.

"I know the feeling. I've been in several accurate recreations, but never the real thing."

"Even as a senator?"

"Few people are permitted to step inside the real Oval Office. Few presidents, even. You start letting presidents in there and the next thing you know, they're trying to use it to impress interns and starlets, and we can't have that. Too much history to defile, you see. You wouldn't believe how many priceless artifacts wouldn't stand up to a simple inspection by black light."

"Surely a president has all the security clearances and access to…"

"We don't do real presidents anymore," said the senator. "We do figureheads. You let someone be president and they start to think they're qualified to make decisions. The continuity of governance would go to hell in a handbasket!"

"Then what are we voting for?"

"A white smile. Straight teeth. Nice hair. Don't pretend it's anything deeper than that when statistics predict the tallest candidate wins most of the time."

"If that's how we pick presidents, how does the president choose an ambassador?"

"Ah, the cat's out of the bag, is it?"

"A little bird may have mentioned it."

"A little court jester, more like. For such a small fellow, Victor Hurley has a big mouth."

"Is it true?"

"It can be," said the senator. "All you have to do is say yes, and you'll be our man in Bahrain. I believe you're familiar with our ally in the Persian Gulf."

"Is saying no an option?"

"No."

"Then my answer is yes."

"I thought you'd see it my way."

"So it's back to Bahrain again," Craig pondered. "When do I leave?"

"Leave?" laughed Senator Wolcott, throwing open an emergency-exit door. "You've already arrived."

The salty smell of the sea hit Craig in the face, and clear blue water was no more than fifty feet away, across a beach of white sand.

20

THE MEDIA WAS EXCITED to land an interview with the nation's newest ambassador about his terrifying experience at the mercy of zealot extremists, but they were told Joseph Kinney was taking the next six to eight weeks to be with his fictional family and was asking for privacy in this trying time. He would make himself available to the press no more than two months from now. That was dozens of news cycles away, and he would be old hat long before that. Just another forgotten ambassador to a country no one had heard of, or could spell if they did.

While he was waiting for Joseph William Kinney's official residence to be readied for him, Craig spent his time walking the many beaches of Durrat Al Bahrain and swimming. He split his time between the sea and hotel pools, depending on whether he was in the mood for salt or chlorine. So far, his official duties had ranged from light to non-existent, and nobody on his assigned staff had been particularly interested in letting him know what was expected of him. Whatever they were doing, they seemed to have things well in hand, so Craig left them to it.

It was during one of his aimless patrols along The Golden Beach that Craig found himself staring at a shapely figure. The shape was truncated, and he knew at once who it belonged to.

Paula Reece was lying back on a reclined chaise lounge. She looked practically naked in a tiny bikini and no prosthetics. The sun had baked on an amber tan, and her callused stumps had arrived at a pleasing almond hue. She looked great, except for the fact that the number of stumps had doubled. Paula, the tanning torso, looked about ready to be flipped over so the sun could even out her backside.

"Oh my God, Paula! What happened to you?" Craig asked, afraid to hear what horrible accident had further maimed her.

Paula looked at him over the rims of her sunglasses and smiled at the unexpected reunion.

"Didn't you hear?" she said. "I'm a media darling now."

"But your arms!"

"Oh these little things?" she said, raising what was left of the two limbs that now ended at the elbow. "It's all good. Purely cosmetic surgery. I was all played out as a double amputee. But things are looking up as a quad. Another nose job, new hair style and dye, and

I'm back on the circuit. This time with a full-time nurse, a press agent, and a business manager."

"You have an entourage now?"

"It's pricey, but I'm raking it in. Twenty-six thousand crowd-funding patrons and counting. Plus personal-appearance fees, Kickstarter projects, and a life story. I'm writing an autobiography about my brave struggle. Dictating, obviously. Lots of fictional facts and memories of things that never happened. I've already sold the screen rights. You'll never guess who's attached to direct."

Craig was pleased for Paula. She seemed happy and prosperous, but he couldn't help but feel a twinge of concern. She was determined to commit to the bit, but the demands of the role were steep.

"What happens when your latest tragedy blows over?" he asked. "You'll never work again."

"Don't be silly. I'm the darling of La La Land. The offers are pouring in. My acting career is off to the races at last. I only had to give an arm and a leg. Two of each, actually."

"Doesn't it limit your roles?"

"With the effects they have these days?" she said, sounding like she would wave away the notion dismissively if she still had hands. "They can CG on as many limbs as they want to. All I have to do is emote for the close-ups."

"I'm glad it's all working out for you."

"How are things on your end?" Paula asked. "I haven't heard a word since you ghosted me."

"I nearly ghosted everybody. But things worked out for me, too, I guess."

"Congratulations," she said. "Welcome back from the dead."

"What are these things?" Craig asked, picking up a couple of curved metal implements stuck on the end of two pilons with adjustable sockets.

"They're transtibial leg blades," said Paula. "Now that I'm rolling in it, I thought I'd splurge on the hot rod of prosthetic legs. Why walk when you can run?"

"I've run enough," said Craig. "I was thinking about taking things slow for a while."

"Want to go for a walk then?"

"You up for that?"

"Some assembly required," said Paula. "My personal assistant is off running errands, but if you help me strap on my gear, we can head out."

There were a couple of prosthetic arms to go with the new legs. One after another, following her instructions for a tight but comfortable fit, Craig assisted Paula until she was equipped with four viable limbs that permitted nearly a full range of movement.

Sitting up, Paula offered Craig a latex hand. It was rubbery but warm from the sun, with enough give to almost feel like flesh and blood. He took it and pulled her to her titanium feet. Together they strolled across the wet sand, leaving two sets of prints, foot and blade, to be washed away in the surf almost as soon as they left their mark.

We get wise by asking questions, and even if these are not answered, we get wise, for a well-packed question carries its answer on its back as a snail carries its shell.

-James Stephens

Acknowledgements

The author wishes to thank Michael Brodie, Ellie Presner, Eric Packman, and Alex Ruaux for their eagle eyes, healthy skepticism, and unhealthy association with the arts.

About the Author

Shane Simmons is an award-winning screenwriter and graphic novelist whose work has appeared in international film festivals, museums, and lectures about design and structure. His art has been discussed in multiple books and academic journals about sequential storytelling, and his short stories have been printed in critically praised anthologies of history, crime, and horror. He was born in Lachine, a suburb of Montreal best known for being massacred in 1689 and having a joke name.

Also by Shane Simmons

Novels

Necropolis
Epitaph
Sex Tape
Filmography

Collections

Raw and Other Stories
Petty Crimes and Vindictive Criminals

Booklets

Carrion Luggage
Choke the Chicken
Hot Pennies
The Red Baron: An Ace for the Ages

Graphic Novels

The Long and Unlearned Life of Roland Gethers
The Failed Promise of Bradley Gethers
The Inauspicious Adventures of Filson Gethers

Author's Note

Small-press publishers rely on reviews from readers like you to help get the word out about their books. Whether it's a simple star rating or a written critique, every bit of feedback helps convince the impersonal computer algorithms of Amazon, and other literary outlets, that the book you just read has merit and deserves more exposure. Please support independent authors, editors, and publishers by taking a few moments to share your thoughts and opinions with other potential readers who may be sitting on the fence about trying an intriguing novel or collection. Your suggestions or comments can make all the difference when it comes to helping them find a new writer they'll like, or matching a struggling author with the readership he or she deserves. Thank you.